BOOK ONE OF THE BIOKIN CHRONICLES

SAPLING'S ORBIT

SPENCER ROSE

SAPLING'S ORBIT

First published in 2021 by Spencer Rose

For more information, email spencer@spencerrosewrites.com

ISBN 978-0-6453613-6-0 (paperback)
ISBN 978-0-6453613-1-5 (digital edition)

2 3 4 5 6 7 8 9 10

Cover Art by Petyr Donat
Cover Design by Sarah Anderson.

spencerrosewrites.com

Books By Spencer Rose

The Biokin Chronicles (reading order):
Sapling's Orbit
Sapling's Aurora
Sapling's Depths
Sapling's Rising

Short Stories

The Urvillion Pass
Starbound Soup

Contents

Blank   VI

One   1

Two   17

Three   27

Four   38

Five   48

Six   54

Seven   65

Eight   73

Nine   84

Ten   97

Eleven   106

Blank   123

Authour's Note

G'day!

This book is written in Australian English, thanks to my English teacher drilling the Aussie spelling of words into my brain from a young age.

This means you might see words spelled according to our language style, such as 'color' written as 'colour', 'realize' as 'realise' and other similar variations.

Enjoy!

Cheers,
Spencer.

One

In the moonlight, the bright red sand of the planet Prema looked purple. I stumbled, gasping for breath, leaning over my knees as I inhaled. A tear was working its way up the hem of my dress. My footprints were scattered across the purple sand behind me, mirroring my wild and desperate footfalls across the desert. Sand was in my socks now, gritty against my feet.

I couldn't see the forest anymore, only the achingly long purple landscape and silent mining machines.

Ahead of me was the faint yellow glow of the train station in the moonlight.

My stomach tightened as I thought I heard voices shouting behind me. Hunting. Searching for us.

My heart was pounding in my chest.

Mila pointed to the platform across the desert, "We need to get there before they do!"

Inhale. Exhale. Inhale. Exhale.

I nodded to Mila and started running again. Running for my life.

Four days earlier

I balanced one foot in the tree branch and the other in the bough, pausing to keep my balance. My fingers tightly gripped a vine that I had looped about the tree trunk as a brace. Looking across the forest canopy, I squinted in the dawn light. My breath created little clouds in the chilly morning air as I sought landmarks. There were tall twin firs to the south, the mountain peak to the north. I recognised a dip in the forest to the east that was the river. To the west stood the city of Tevinter. It was all glass, metal, and skyscrapers. The forest ended abruptly, like a giant had drawn a line between the city and forest as far as the eye could see. I always used the tallest tower in Tevinter, shaped like a bird's feather, as my landmark reference.

I pulled a map of waxy paper out of my hessian backpack and looked where we were in relation to those landmarks. We were right where we were meant to be.

I called down to Perse, far below me, "It's got to be here!"

"What?" the old woman called, straining to hear.

"We're in the right place!" I confirmed as I slung the vine that I was using for support down the tree trunk. I leaned my weight into the vine, and I began to walk down the trunk until I reached the next branch down.

"Where is it then?" she called. Then, pursing her lips, she muttered, "Let's do this the old-fashioned way!". Perse sat right down in the leaf litter of the forest, letting out a groan as she sat on her bad hip.

As I clambered down, my long woolen skirt began to block my view of the branches for footholds. I grabbed the brown fabric and twisted it between my legs, tying a large knot. I remembered the way Sabine had used to tease me, "Just wear trousers!" she'd say, leaping from branch to branch. "It's what everyone off-world wears!"

"I don't care what everyone off-world wears!" I'd shot back, "I *like* my dress!". It was times like these that I regretted not trying trousers even once.

As I reached the lowest limbs of the tree, Perse was meditating below me. She sat cross-legged, eyes closed, in her own blue wool-spun dress. I hadn't noticed the flower she'd tucked into her tight grey bun until I was standing above her. She sat silently, breathing steadily. While I couldn't see it, I knew she was linked with the forest, following the connections between the trees all around us.

"Aha!" she cried sharply, her eyes snapping open. Perse pointed to a tree a few metres away, with a vine wrapped about its roots, blocking the base of the tree. "In there!"

I jumped to the forest floor and looped the vine about my waist should I need it later. I helped Perse stand. She let out a soft moan as she put weight on her hip. Perse grabbed a nearby branch as a walking stick and hobbled over to the tree she'd pointed to. She cleared away the vine, revealing a hollow in the tree roots. Inside were seven yellow-veined mushrooms, larger than my hand.

"Perfect!" she whispered.

She started to lean over to pick them, but started exhaling sharply, clutching her hip.

"Addison? Can you–?" she gestured to the mushrooms.

I crouched over the mushrooms. I plucked just two and placed them in Perse's basket.

"And why didn't you take all of them?" she quizzed me. I rolled my eyes because I was old enough to not need lessons anymore. But dutifully, I responded.

"We only take what we need," I recited her lessons, "And so the mushrooms will be here next year,"

She nodded sharply, then asked, "And how many credits does one of these mushrooms get at the markets in Tevinter?"

My skin became hot. "How many... *credits*?" I asked, ensuring I heard her correctly.

Perse nodded, keeping her eyes fixed on me.

"We—we don't use credits," I stammered. Was it a trick question? My mind raced. When we were young, we went on a school trip into the city of Tevinter to visit an art museum. We saw people tapping devices together to exchange 'credits'. But in our village of Nimbaii, we didn't use credits. We did occasionally trade at the market, yes, but not for credits.

"We don't use credits in Nimbaii," Perse agreed, "Because the forest provides for us. We look after it, and it looks after us." she gently patted the trunk of a nearby tree. "But when we leave the village, we have to use credits to buy food and shelter. And having some idea of how much things cost is a useful skill."

I knew why she'd brought this conversation up today. Because it was my birthday. Soon, I would need to understand how credits worked.

"So, how many credits is a mushroom worth?" I ventured.

Perse shrugged. "An ordinary mushroom? Might be a single credit," she explained. "An apple might be two credits."

She held up the mushroom in her hand. "*This* mushroom? Four *hundred* credits."

I frowned. "Why is this mushroom worth so much?"

"Because something is worth more credits if it's rare. *This* mushroom is tough to find. In fact, there are only two people on this planet who know where to find it." She pointed to herself and back to me.

"Oh," I said, understanding. "Because only biokin are allowed in our forest?"

She nodded.

"This mushroom is very rare. We're the only ones who have access to it. And we could get a lot of credits for it if we sold it."

"What would we need credits for?" I asked. "Don't we get everything we need from the forest?"

"Well, *almost* everything," she winked. "The elders do keep credits aside for some things. We can't, for example, make our own navcomms."

"But we don't use credits, so we don't need navcomms," I said, thinking of that small device I'd seen people using in Tevinter.

"When you're in the forest, you don't need it," Perse nodded, "But when you are off-world, you will."

My breath left me. "So, I will get one? For my pilgrimage?"

"Yes, you will get your very own."

My heart began to race. I wasn't ready for my pilgrimage. Even though it was my birthday. I was meant to be prepared. But travelling on my own to another planet for a year? It was exciting, but terrifying at the same time. Like jumping off a waterfall and not being sure how deep the water was at the bottom.

"Perse?" I asked, my voice small, "What did you do on your pilgrimage?"

She stood still, her eyes lost in the forest. I was about to repeat myself, but then she spoke. "You've spent your whole life in this forest, Addison. At sixteen, you are old enough to see the universe and to find out if this life here, as a biokin, is what you want. You might want to find a new home out in the world. Or you might return to this forest. What I discovered out there was very different from what you may discover out there. But that's the point. Everyone's pilgrimage is different, but the purpose is the same. To find yourself."

The chill breeze hit me then. For the first time in my life, I noticed how impossibly tall the trees were around me.

Perse looked up at the rising sun. "We'd better get going. You'll be late for school. What's left on the list?"

I pulled out the waxy map and saw two more plants we needed to find.

"Cat's claw is next."

"Thank the Ancients," she muttered, rubbing her hip. It reduced inflammation, so I imagined she would start peeling the vine and chewing it as soon as she laid eyes on it.

"And what tree does the cat's claw vine usually cling to?"

I knew the answer to that one. It had saved my life when I was twelve. I'd been out foraging, and I'd twisted my ankle. Finding the cat's claw was the only way I could make it home. "Kember oak."

"And where will we find it?"

"South of the mountain."

"We might just make a healer of you one day!" she cried, grinning as she began ambling down the mountain with newfound energy.

I followed her, feeling like my heart had separated from my body. I could see my future if it was here in Nimbaii. I would become the village healer. I would be a good healer, too. I studied hard and did my best to learn as much as I could from Perse. But would I discover another life in the stars? I'd soon find out.

***

I sat in the leaf litter on the forest floor. I loved that earthy smell. The leaves felt like a blanket against the damp soil. I leaned my back against a tree, and the rough bark dug into my back. My woolen dress rubbed against my skin. The air didn't hurt my lungs as it had earlier in the morning, but it was still cool. The breeze brought leaves and twigs down from great heights, and birds scattered at predators that only they could see.

I exhaled slowly. And then I inhaled, counting to three.

I settled my attention on my breath in and out. In and out. And I expanded my awareness to focus on the world around me. My body sank into the dirt as I listened to the forest. Rustling leaves, a bird squawking and flapping away, making a branch high above rustle. I had the smell of earth in my nostrils and the taste of my morning coffee on my lips. And I rested my fingers on the tree roots next to me. And I connected with the forest.

In my mind's eye, the tree I was touching lit up like a firefly. I could see down into its roots in my mind, and I sunk deep into the soil and then I tapped into the tree next to it. And then the one next to that. Even the tiny vines springing from the forest floor lit up, phosphorescent.

I was *listening* to the forest. It sighed and swayed. I knew which trees were craving sun and which plants were hounded by bugs. I knew which saplings were getting strangled by vines. I saw which evergreens were strong and tall, ready to share their nutrients with the plants around them. It was like I was being bathed in sunlight when I linked with the forest.

I expanded the reach of my mind in a circle about me, tapping each plant as I went, seeing if I could find the dew twine plant. I expanded my search, tapping more and more plants, but not finding the tree. The forest lit up, tree by tree, plant by plant, as I extended my reach in my vision. I tried to expand my mind out wider—but I hit a mental block. I couldn't reach out any further. I wanted to push wider—but my attention wavered, and my circle shrunk back a few metres as I struggled to hold it. I tried one last time, pushing my reach another metre, two, further and further, connecting with more shrubs until—yes!—the dew twine on the very edge of my consciousness. I could feel some warm sunlight from a gap in the trees above it. I could sense the plant was content, not yearning for water or sun. It was at peace—exactly how we wanted the plants in the forest to feel. My reach into the forest snapped back as, in exhaustion, I disconnected.

I opened my eyes, letting the real-world morning sun flood my vision. The trees ahead of me returned with a mosaic of leaf litter in reds and browns on the forest floor.

"Well?" Perse asked, sitting across from me.

"Up the mountain," I said, trying to hide my exhaustion. "Near the big Markson tree."

"Oh?" Perse raised her eyebrows. "That's quite a reach."

"I've been practising," I shrugged. I didn't tell her I had been sneaking out at night with Lian. He was convinced Sabine had left a stash of moonshine in a nearby cave. We'd each extended our reach in different directions, trying to map the underground. So far, we'd had no success, but Lian kept insisting we head out after dark.

I stood up, feeling a little lightheaded, and handed Perse her walking stick.

"Perse, where did you find the ship to take you on your pilgrimage?" I asked.

"Not that you'd believe these old bones," she smiled wickedly, "But I used to be quite a looker. So, I walked right into the tavern on the edge of Tevinter—I think it was called *The Fox Paw*—and announced that I needed a ride out of the solar system. I had three offers by dawn—including one for marriage."

"So, what happened?"

"Well, none of them turned up at the spaceport the next day! Too much cider, I suspect. So, in the end, I had to convince a wheat merchant to take me. I told him I could get rid of the rats on his ship if he gave me a passage to the next planet. He thought I could talk to the wheat, you know, and get it to 'expel the rats'. I'm not quite sure what that meant considering we can only connect with living plants, but it got me a passage."

"Could you find the rats?"

"I was a stellar aim with a slingshot; I'll have you know." Perse winked.

"I'll watch out!" I laughed.

***

I sat at my school desk, squirming. It was childish, but the last thing I wanted to do on my birthday was to be in school. I was like a dog tied to a tree; all I craved was to run outside. I wished I could head down to the river with Lian and jump off the highest rock into the depths below. I would lie in the sun and daydream about what life would be like off-world. Outside the classroom window, the younger students were on their lunch break. They ran about the village, playing hide and seek in the square, darting amongst the houses, climbing trees, throwing a ball about. How I craved to be out there instead of in this classroom.

In complete contrast to my itchy feet, Lian was asleep right next to me. His head was in his arms, his light brown hair fell over his eyes as his enormous arms cocooned his face into a makeshift pillow. Some of the younger girls near me cooed when they saw him asleep, but I just rolled my eyes. If they knew how much of a dork he was, they wouldn't be fawning over him. I'd once seen him strip off his trousers when a frog took refuge in there during a sudden thunderstorm, and I tell you what, there was truly nothing to fuss about. I imagined one day I'd find someone worthy of swooning over. I just wouldn't find them here in Nimbaii.

I gently nudged Lian's ankle with my foot, and when he didn't wake, I kicked him.

He started, and some drool stuck to his notebook.

"We're about to learn about the solar system," I whispered with gentle sarcasm because every year a student had to do this same presentation.

"Oh, goody," Lian said, blinking awake. "Are we learning about all of it this time?"

I shook my head, "Not likely."

He'd been referring to Sabine's anger a few years ago that we only learned about the planets with biokin on them. "How does this help us on pilgrimage?" she'd complained. "How am I meant to prepare for my trip if I don't even know about other planets?"

At the time, I'd just shrugged, partly because I didn't like causing a fuss and also because my pilgrimage had seemed a lifetime away. But, today, I had butterflies in my stomach because it was already time for my pilgrimage. And now *I* was wondering why we only learned about planets with biokin on them and not the rest of them.

Kimonee, a younger girl in the class, stood at the front, hands quivering. I strained to hear her quiet voice as she read in a monotone from her paper. As the senior students, Lian and I needed to at least feign interest so the poor thing could survive the stress of public speaking.

"A long time ago, all biokin were on one planet," Kimonee stuttered, "We lived in harmony with nature and were protected by the Ancient Tree. But then, one day, the biokin saw an asteroid nearing their planet. The tree told them to shelter in the roots, and it grew cocoons for all the villagers–"

Lian raised an eyebrow at me and whispered, "This is getting a little into the realm of mythology, isn't it?"

"Oh, lay off it, Lian, she's trying," I whispered back.

"–and when the asteroid hit, all the biokin were scattered across the galaxy, protected by the cocoons. We landed on several planets and grew into peaceful communities like the one we live in here."

Our teacher nodded enthusiastically, and Kimonee continued, "I will now share a summary of all the planets that biokin live on, starting with ours."

"Oh, come on. We live here. We know this one!" Lian muttered. He rolled his eyes and folded his arms into a makeshift pillow again.

I truly began to wonder then, with a pang of anxiety, what was on the other planets. I didn't know much about them at all. Some were habitable and had humans. While we learned about the other biokin planets, hundreds of other worlds were in this sector. Where would I go on my pilgrimage? What would I see? Perse wasn't helpful at all when I asked her about her time off-world. I sighed. I supposed the only way I was going to find out what life was like offworld was to go. The knot in my stomach tightened.

***

The bonfire was taller than me, even standing on my tip-toes. A plume of smoke wound up to the star-studded night, and music filled the air. Smoke filled my nose with an earthy, sooty smell. I loved that smell. It reminded me of midnight dances, laughter, and family.

The bonfire was across the town square, and our village surrounded us. In the moonlight, our homes might have looked like they were strange trees from the heart of the forest. A passerby would not guess that the living buildings started as saplings woven together to grow into beautiful homes over a generation. My mother worked in the village as an architect, helping grow a new set of homes that would, in a few years, be the homes of the next generation in the town. We had drawings all over our house, including designs and city maps from Tevinter. She always said that just because we didn't live the same way as people outside the forest, there was no reason we couldn't learn from them. She also hoped, I suspected, that they would also one day come to learn from us.

I looked back toward the bonfire, and in the coals, one of the elders of the village roasted beets, mushrooms, and spiced chickpeas in an enormous cauldron. He served the feast out into small clay bowls, handing them out to revelers.

Most of the village was here for the celebration, including Perse. My parents danced together by the bonfire like they were young again. I rolled my eyes but secretly loved how they always made each other laugh with their dancing.

I sat by Lian on a log overlooking the fire. I was eating the spicy warm beets with relish.

"Did you get anything for your birthday from your parents?" He asked, picking at his own bowl, avoiding the chickpeas.

"I did," Leaning over, like I had a secret, I whispered, "I got a navcomm."

His eyebrows rose. "*Seriously?*"

I nodded, beaming. I had attached it to a leather cord and wore it as a necklace tucked into my dress. I pulled it out, showing the small metal device, no larger than my thumb. "It's for my pilgrimage."

"Do you have any credits on it?" He asked, eyes wide.

I nodded. "I have two hundred credits. Dad says that's enough to get a fare off-world. Or get some warm clothes if I go somewhere with snow. It's enough to start until I find a job or something and I can get more credits."

"Where will you go?"

"Well, absolutely not one of the biokin planets," I answered, rolling my eyes. "Kimonee's report was so detailed that it was like being there, so I don't feel the need to go at all."

He laughed, and as I met his eyes, my heart jumped to my throat. Fear. Fear of leaving him. Of travelling to the unknown.

There was a commotion across the bonfire. Someone was hitting a spoon to a saucepan like a bell. My mother stood up on a log, clearly intending to make a birthday speech for me. I flushed but knew that this was part of birthday traditions. I walked over to her and stood by her as a circle stood by to listen to the speech. Lian and my father hovered nearby.

"Thank you for attending our little celebration," she said. "I cannot believe my baby girl has come of age!"

My father lifted his glass with a cheer, "Happy birthday, Addison!"

"Now, we know Addison is due to leave soon on her pilgrimage, and she'll be gone a whole year! I cannot wait to hear of her adventures and see the person she becomes after her year away." My mother's voice cracked as she inhaled. "But she isn't leaving just yet! The first step of the pilgrimage is to get a ship off-world—and she doesn't have one yet–"

"Do you, Addison?" My father asked cautiously.

I laughed and shook my head, "Not yet, Dad," and he theatrically sighed with relief.

"While she's still here, let us all celebrate this day and make the most of our time together! Let's dance and enjoy the feast!"

The crowd applauded, and as they dispersed, Perse pulled me aside.

"I've got a little gift for you for your travels, Addison."

She handed me a small envelope. Inside was a set of seeds. Some I recognised, and I knew they were rare. "May these help you on your journey. Remember that we all change. It can be hard to grow and change. Sometimes we feel like nothing is happening, but all that energy results in a beautiful transformation in time. Like a seed into a sunflower. Be open to the transformation."

"Thanks, Perse." I tucked her seeds into my pocket and gave her a long hug.

"Okay," she said after a moment, "This old duck needs to have her beauty rest."

I clasped her hand. "Thanks, Perse. For everything."

"Don't wait too long to go on your pilgrimage, Addison. It's better for the soul to do it sooner rather than later."

The drumming circle started again. My father pulled my mother into a dance again, and as I watched them, they offered for me to join the dance. I shook my head. Tonight, I did not feel like dancing. I headed back to my spot by the fire with Lian.

"You know, I have a gift for you too," he said, voice taut.

"You do?" I asked, surprised. "It's not beetles again?"

He shook his head, noticeably silent, eyes averted. He handed me a small cloth bag. From inside, I pulled a thin, woven bracelet. It was blue with red stones threaded through. The stones sparkled in the firelight.

"It's beautiful! Where did you get this?" I held out my wrist so he could tie it fast.

"I made it," he said sheepishly, fumbling with the tie. "I actually only just finished it at two this morning. It's to give you something to remember me by. Or remember, um, the village. You know. When you're away," he stammered.

"Oh, Lian!" I cried, giving him a hug. "How could I forget you?"

"Well," he shrugged awkwardly, "just in case."

I flushed, feeling that this hug was intimate in a way we hadn't ever been before. I broke off the hug and sat up, feigning another look at the bracelet.

"I don't even have transport off-world," I reassured him.

"I am glad you're not leaving immediately," he said quietly.

I sat, watching the bonfire sparks rise to the sky.

"It's not like you'll be here on your own without me for long anyway," I said. "You're almost sixteen, too. You'll be on your own pilgrimage in a few weeks."

He let out a long, slow sigh, like the sigh of life racing along before we were ready.

"Are you scared?" he asked, and it sounded like he was asking more for himself than for me.

"A little bit. A little excited, too. Mostly just worried that I won't know what to do. That I'll make a silly mistake and end up in trouble."

"Like what?"

"Like, everywhere else uses credits, and I don't even know how they work."

Lian's eyes lit up, "Let's practise!"

I laughed, "Practice? Practice what?"

"Using credits," he leapt up and grabbed a nearby stick. "Here, here, buy this from me!"

I couldn't help but laugh and looked about the bonfire to ensure that no one was close enough to witness this embarrassing charade. "Okay, okay, um, can I buy that stick for, um, ten credits?" I asked, holding up my navcomm on my lanyard.

Lian frowned. I laughed even harder. "You need a navcomm. And we tap them together to transfer the credits."

I found a rock of adequate size and handed it to him. "Here, that's your navcomm."

He laughed, and we gently tapped the navcomm and the rock together, meeting eyes. My heart skipped a beat.

"Thanks for your business. Please come again," he said, handing me the stick.

He pointed to some mushrooms on my plate. "Can I buy that mushroom for, um, one hundred credits?"

"No, no," I said, remembering my conversation with Perse. "A mushroom is only one credit. But you can pay a hundred if you like," I winked.

"How do you know how much things are?" he asked, looking cheated as if I'd been studying in secret.

"Perse told me this morning," I explained, "But only about mushrooms and apples."

Lian folded his arms. "This is so unfair. What if I did that for real? If I bought a mushroom for a hundred credits instead of one. I'd be out of money in a day! Isn't there somewhere we can go and like, buy an apple, and see how it's done?"

Only Ancient Ones know what inspired me to say what I said next. Perhaps it was the high of my birthday celebration. Maybe it was the fact that I was on the precipice of change, anyway.

"There is a place," I said, keeping my voice low. "We can't buy an apple, but we can buy an apple cider."

"I'm listening," murmured Lian, keeping his posture casual, his eyes remaining on the fire as if we were discussing the weather.

"We'd need to sneak out because it's outside the forest. It's called *The Fox Paw.*

Two

T he moon was high in the sky. Lian and I marched through the forest. He'd changed into a cream-coloured tunic and brown trousers, with a blue jacket over the top. "Addi, we are going to stand out as biokin if we wear what we usually wear in Nimbaii," he explained. It still wasn't anything like the outfits the people in Tevinter wore, which were shiny like spider silk.

"I think it will be pretty obvious that we're biokin when we walk out of the forest," I shot back, but I had changed my outfit, too. I wore my favourite green wool dress, with a cream shawl wrapped about my shoulders.

The shortest route to the city of Tevinter usually took about forty minutes to walk from our village, so we ran the first leg, half out of excitement, and half so we couldn't change our minds. Within a half-hour, we were on the border of the forest.

Ahead of us, instead of old trees blocking out the sky, skyscrapers hid the stars. We found the fence that bordered our forest and followed it north until we reached the main gate. It felt wildly rebellious to step from the forest to the road outside without a teacher or parent with us. The sign we passed read: *Nimbaii Forest Reserve. Biokin access only.*

Outside of the forest was a quiet road with a few houses and small plots of land for farming. Streetlights lit the road, and I squinted in their strange false light.

We started walking faster in anticipation and then burst into a run as we headed into the streets.

"Where is it?" Lian asked, looking about.

"It's around here. Don't you remember passing it when we went to the art gallery?"

"No! Do you?" he asked incredulously.

"Yes. The walls are covered with space women."

"Space women?" He asked, raising an eyebrow.

"Well, you'll see when we get there!" I shot back, flushing.

We followed the thump of bass through the streets, and as we continued past the houses, finally saw the bright lights outside the tavern. It was no longer called *The Fox Paw* as in Perse's day, but *The Thirsty Captain*. The walls outside the bar were plastered with photos of spaceships and women wearing clothing that looked much more practical for swimming than for space travel.

Two men stood at the door as security. They were tall and muscular. The one with a moustache leaned to the other and murmured, "Are biokin even allowed out of the forest?"

The other rolled his eyes, "Of course they are. They just *like it* there, so they can be *one with the forest*." He had said 'one with the forest' in a mocking voice.

At this, I hesitated. I looked to Lian for reassurance. He nodded encouragement for me to continue. I stepped toward the men.

"Hi," I said, "We'd like an apple cider."

The man with the moustache stifled his laughter, and the other spoke very slowly, enunciating each word. "You order inside at the bar. We just check how old you are. You need to be fifteen to enter." He held up a small metal device with red lights and explained, "You put your thumb against it. We check your DNA to see your age."

I put my thumb to the device. "Ouch," I complained at the pin-prick, but the device lit up green.

Lian followed suit, and it also lit up green.

"You're old enough," said the clean-shaven man. "Do you know that you need credits to buy drinks here? Do you have credits?"

I held up my lanyard with my navcomm. "I have two hundred credits," I announced. "Will that be enough?"

The man with the moustache laughed and confirmed, "It will be enough. And if you keep announcing how many credits you have, you'll make friends really quickly here!"

I stepped past them and opened the door to the tavern.

The room inside was crowded, with people yelling across the music to each other, spilling drinks and jostling, knocking into nearby pa-trons. Posters were all over the walls of women in swimming costumes riding toy rockets. Vidscreens were high overhead and showed women dancing on a beach, but it didn't seem to sync at all with fast-paced music that was blasting all around. The lights were low, and it was hard to see inside, and the smell of beer made it hard to breathe. The carpet was sticky from decades of drinks spilled on the floor.

Lian put his hand on my arm to not lose me in the throng as I worked my way towards the bar. As I approached, some of the men looked me up and down, and one exclaimed, "Oh, ho! Look what we have here!"

I supposed they hadn't seen a biokin in the flesh, but I didn't like the way they looked at me. Like I was meat. Lian clutched my arm even more tightly as we wove our way through the crowd.

"Well, shall we give this a go?" Lian asked, leaning close to be heard over the din.

I nodded, and we lined up. The service area was surrounded by men of all skin colours who wore old, torn jumpsuits covered in oil and paint. Above the music, they shouted insults about slow ships and their parentage, which was met with laughter by others who got the jokes.

I stood on my tip-toes to watch how the others in the bar were paying. I realised I looked silly, but I figured it was better to look stupid now than later.

Ahead of me stood a girl about my age who wore her tattered blue jumpsuit tied at the waist, with a black singlet underneath. She didn't look much older than me. Obviously, she was familiar with queues in bars because she was impatiently tapping her navcomm against her leg. I wondered if what she wore was the fashion with women off-world. Her black, curly hair was tied in a messy ponytail and she had lean muscular arms, which surprised me as I had always thought offworlders just, well, floated about in space and didn't need much strength.

A man next to her leaned over towards her, "You want a ride?"

She ignored him, waiting for the barman to serve her, hand still tapping on her leg. So, the man grabbed her shoulder, "Hey," he said, "Do you want a ride off-world?"

Annoyed, she rolled her eyes. "I have a ride."

"My ride is better," he growled with a wink.

She ignored him and turned to the barman, "Scotch. Neat." She held up her navcomm and tapped it against a small machine the barman held out. The red light on the machine turned green as the payment was processed, and she pocketed the device.

"You old enough to be in here?" the barman asked.

"Security let me in here, didn't they?"

The barman shrugged and served her up an amber drink in a small glass.

She took a sip, exhaled, and stretched her neck and shoulders.

The man next to her continued, "So, what about it? You want to see my ride?"

She finally turned to him and said, "I don't need to ride in the cargo hold. I have my own ship."

The man blanched. Without another word, she worked her to the back of the bar, and sat at an empty booth.

My mouth was hanging open a little. Women could own ships?

The barman called to me, "What do you want?"

"Me? I will have two ciders!" I held up two fingers.

"Ten credits," the barman said. He held up the little machine and, hesitantly, I mashed my navcomm against the device until the red lights turned green. "You're good," he nodded to my navcomm, and I realised the payment had been processed. He poured the ciders, and I tucked the navcomm back into my dress. I made a mental note of the price of cider. Five credits each. I was doing the math already: were the two hundred credits my parents gave me really going to be enough to get me off-world?

Lian picked up his cider and pointed to a vacant booth at the back.

We worked our way through the boisterous crowd, trying to avoid adding our cider to the sticky floor beneath our feet as the elbows of the crowd knocked against us. We passed people leaning over low tables, arm wrestling, and in the back corner, men and women danced slowly.

Lian and I crawled into the booth, knees knocking against each other.

"Cheers," he said, holding his glass up, and then at my frown he explained, "It's what you say when you drink cider. According to Sabine." He clinked his glass against mine.

"Cheers," I sipped. My mouth exploded with the tartness, and the bubbles made my eyes water. I coughed as I swallowed. Lian blinked, trying to stop coughing himself, and we both laughed.

"Maybe we should have ordered that other drink that girl ordered," Lian suggested. I nodded, but was unsure it would be any better.

I was keenly aware that his warm knees were pressed upright against mine.

"Now you've practised using your navcomm," Lian said, "you're ready to start your pilgrimage. You are of age. You've got your navcomm. Do you need anything else?"

"Well, perhaps a ride on a ship?" I laughed.

He pointed out the man at the bar, "That guy sounds like he's got a ride on a ship."

I wrinkled my nose. "I don't want to go on a ship with that guy."

"What about that girl?" Lian asked, scanning the bar for her. "She's got a ship, too."

My stomach dropped. "What?"

"Well, why don't you ask her to take you off-world?"

"She seems a little...." I couldn't think of the word. "Direct?"

He took a sip of cider, shrugging.

"But seriously, if you're going to go on pilgrimage, this is a good place to find a ship," he said.

I sighed, "That's what Perse said."

He almost choked on his drink. "Perse? *Perse* told you to come here and get a ship?" As I nodded, Lian looked to the ceiling dramatically, "Oh, Ancient ones, help us all. If you're getting advice from Perse, how are you going to get off-world? She's about four hundred years old." He finished his drink in one gulp and said, standing, "I'm going to ask that girl for you."

"You're going to *what*?" I asked, leaping to my feet to stop him.

"Well, *you* ask then," he sat back down, gesturing for me to go.

Embarrassed, I squirmed out of the booth and casually scanned the room. The girl was a few booths away. My mouth was dry.

"You can get passage on a ship with her, or you can go with one of these men," he said, waving a hand in the general direction of the men spitting and roughhousing in the bar.

I stepped towards her, hesitantly and exhaled. *Time to be an adult,* I thought to myself. *It's just a question. That's all you're doing. Asking a question.*

The girl was watching people over her glass. She looked me up and down with her green eyes as I approached, no doubt taking in my hand-woven outfit.

"Hi," I ventured cautiously. The girl didn't respond but met my gaze, so I continued, heart racing. "I'm looking for someone to take me off-world. I heard you have a ship. I am going on a pilgrimage–"

She folded her arms, muscles taut. "I don't take passengers."

"Oh." Well, that answers that. I slunk back to Lian, face burning.

"That was a little embarrassing," I said, clambering back into the booth.

"It sure was," said Lian, trying not to laugh. "What kind of sales pitch was that? You could have told her you'd pay her!"

I shrugged, "I just didn't know what to say!"

"There are plenty more fish in the river," he said, gesturing towards the bar.

I sighed and put my head in my hands. "I don't think I can go through that again."

"You don't need to find someone tonight."

"Perse said it's better to get it out of the way sooner rather than later."

"I can't believe you're getting all your life advice from Perse," he said, smiling, "But she's right. Besides, the sooner you go, the sooner you'll be back. I'm about to go on my pilgrimage too, so if we both go, we'll both be back at the same time."

"Well, that assumes I'm coming back,"

His smile dropped. "What do you mean?"

I shrugged, "Well, the point of the pilgrimage. To see what is out there in the universe. Maybe there's something else out there for me. Another kind of life. I just don't know yet."

"I—I thought you'd come back," he said, swallowing hard, "for me."

... *What?*

My heart started pounding. This booth felt too small. Lian's legs were squished up against mine. The music was too loud, and people were everywhere. My breaths were quick and shallow.

"For you?" I echoed, feeling like I was disconnected from my body.

"I mean... If you want. We could, you know," he looked at the table, "be betrothed."

I blanched. *"What?"*

Was Lian–who put frogs in my boots and flicked seeds into my dress in class–asking me to marry him? And then, like a dam bursting, I noticed all the little things I'd never paid attention to before. It was Lian who read my favourite books with me by the river. Lian, who wove flowers into my hair for midsummer feast and Lian, who dragged me into the forest in the dead of night, giggling as we searched for lost moonshine. Lian, who spent weeks braiding a bracelet for me.

"Only if you want," he stammered. "I just thought that–" he exhaled, running his hands through his hair, "This wasn't how I meant to say this..."

"I..." My mouth felt dry. "I need to think about it. I don't know what will happen after the pilgrimage. Who I will be. Or who you will be." I was trying to sound reasonable, but I was not making sense. My fingers clutched at my knees. "Lian, you're my best friend. But betrothal is a big thing."

He bit his lip, "I shouldn't have said anything,"

"No–it's fine," I said, quickly, "I just–need time to think."

My face felt hot, and this bar was now so, so small.

"I should go," he said, standing.

"No, Lian, it's okay," I flushed. "Let's just–have another cider."

"I think I've had enough," he said, "I need to clear my head. I'm heading home."

"Lian!" I called as he worked his way through the crowd toward the exit. "Lian!"

Cripes, I thought. *Have I just lost my best friend?*

"Hecking heck," I swore. How could I have been such a fool?

I gulped down air and tried to work through what had just happened. But, I mean, I was right, wasn't I? It seemed foolish to do something like agreeing to marriage when we were both about to go on the biggest trip of our lives where we had no idea where we'd end up.

My insides felt hollow.

I stood and worked my way over to the bar. Since I was here, I may as well try another cider. Or perhaps I'd try that other drink that girl with the ship was drinking. Scotch.

As I neared the bar, I noticed the navcomms in the room buzzed about me at once. The patrons grabbed their devices and started reading the message, a murmuring spreading across the bar.

A man behind me grunted to his friend, "There's new job alert,"

I heard a loud noise near the entrance. One of the barmen was banging a ladle on a frypan, calling for attention. It was like a strange repetition of just a few hours earlier, where I'd sat with my best friend by the bonfire. Which I might never do again.

The bar quietened down, and the burly barman with a short beard climbed onto a chair so we could see him across the bar. "Okay, people. I'm sure most of you have seen the alert that there is a job going around. I'm here in my capacity as a Witness to keep this friendly." He held up an identification badge from his pocket, which was a little metal shield on it. Someone turned down the music. "As you would have seen, the alert is from the company Evo. They want one of those biokin as a consultant for a day to help with a project of theirs'. They've got a thousand credits to whoever can bring the one up to their spacestation tomorrow."

It was news to me that a spacestation was in orbit, but everyone else here seemed very aware of it. Their eyes bulged at the mention of a thousand credits. And in a moment, all eyes on the bar were on me. They were looking for a biokin, and here one was, ready for the taking. The hairs at the back of my neck stood up as an icy fear rose in my chest.

Three

I f everyone in the bar wanted a thousand credits, I was their prize. My heart started to race. Every patron in the tavern looked about, sizing each other up. If this was going to turn into a brawl, I was in the centre of it.

A large man standing directly behind me called out to the room, locking eyes onto the people surrounding us, daring them to speak. "The biokin girl is mine!"

Some men spat on the ground, but no one objected.

He stepped towards me, and I, shaking, took a step to the side and ran into a man there who was cracking his knuckles. It was the same man who had looked me up and down earlier. *Oh, Ancients, help me.* I looked toward the exit, and it was blocked by a crowd of burly men, poised to see how this would play out. I was trapped.

The only sound was a fan, high overhead, whirring in an off-kilter circle.

And then the girl with the dark curly hair spoke. She was talking to the large man behind me, but her voice rang across the bar, "I've got some terrible news for you."

She strode across the room towards the big man, and the crowd parted for her. "I spoke to this biokin earlier and discussed her transport off-world," That was a loose interpretation of events, but one I wasn't going to counter at this exact moment. Then she said something that surprised me. "And we agreed that she's a passenger on my ship."

The man turned to look down at the girl, who was a good head shorter than him. He laughed, a throaty laugh, with spittle flying across the room. "I think that is very unlike–"

She stomped on his foot, and as he recoiled in pain, she pulled one arm behind his back and had a knife at his throat in seconds.

Everyone in the room shuffled back. But no one stepped forward to defend this burly man. It seemed he had no friends on this planet.

"What are you–" he began to rage, but she pressed the knife closer to his throat, a thin bead of blood trickling from his neck. He stopped talking.

"Now that you're willing to have a conversation like a gentleman, shall we ask the lady who she wishes to travel with?"

Again, everyone's eyes fell on me.

"Do you still want a place on my ship?" her eyes bored into mine.

My heart was racing, but I didn't know what choice I had. It seemed someone in this bar was going to take me to this Evo spacestation. And this girl seemed the best option by far. She may have been holding a knife, but she didn't look at me like a piece of meat. My lips felt dry.

She stepped closer to me, dragging the large man with her as the knife left a distinct impression in his skin. She spoke loudly, so everyone could hear.

"I'm your transport," she said, nodding as if willing me to agree with her. And then, to counter my hesitation, she added, "What if we split the credits? 500 each."

My breath caught. I did, I suppose, need credits. And a way off-world. And I figured the alternative was being shoved into someone's cargo hold up to Evo. "Agreed." I said, my voice wobbly, "You are my transport."

She unhinged the man's arm and threw him on the ground, tucking her knife away.

The barman on the stool called across the room, "The job has been agreed to. I witness this event." The crowd started yelling, but he shouted over them, "You know how this works people, we're keeping this clean!"

He pulled out a tablet from his apron, leaning over to the girl with the knife. "This is the contract."

She strode over and inserted her thumbprint in the base of the tablet.

***

I burst out of the tavern into the chill night air. After the contract had been signed, no one was interested in us anymore. I took some deep breaths in the evening air to try to calm down. The sound of cicadas echoed around us. My hands were shaking from the exchange. What the fudge had just happened?

The girl followed me out of the tavern. "Hey," she called.

"You're solid for the trip tomorrow?"

"Yes," I said, heart beating. Of course, I had a lot to do before then, but yes, it was possible.

"You said you wanted transport anyway, right? So where are you heading?"

"Anywhere off-world will do. I'm going on a pilgrimage."

She levelled her gaze at me. "A *pilgrimage*?" She put her hands on her hips. "Look, I can get you to the Evo spacestation and then transport you to the next planet I'm heading to. But it's not free. There are docking costs on each planet. So, I need 300 credits if you want me to take you any further."

"Okay," I said. I did the math. I knew I had just under 200 credits on my navcomm from the cider. And I would get 500 credits from this

Evo job if we split the credits. More than enough for the 300 credit docking costs I owed her.

"We'll meet at the spaceport in Tevinter tomorrow at noon."

She held my gaze for a second, thinking something through. And then, resolved, she turned to walk away.

"Wait!" I called.

She spun back around.

"Thank you," I said, "Those men were..."

She nodded to the knife at her waist, "I know what those men are like."

"And, well, thank you for the ride. I know you don't take passengers, but I appreciate it."

"I need to get to the Evo spacestation, anyway. I have an errand to run there. But it's, you know, invite-only, so your invite is my invite."

Well, that explained her sudden interest in helping me. Either way, she was my ride off-world.

"I'm Addison," I said, and I held out a hand to shake.

"Mila," she replied without shaking my hand and resumed walking away. Then, she called out behind her, "Tomorrow, at noon, don't be late!"

I exhaled and looked up at the stars. *Ancients tell me what happened tonight?* Tomorrow, I'd be looking at the stars from right up there with them.

***

The forest was dark compared to the brightly lit city. But I'd walked this forest since I was a child, and I knew the landmarks, even at night. I'd memorised the big old trees that served as markers, with wood that seemed bright white at night. I knew where the path had ditches that we would leap over by day and where the stray tree roots would trip you up if you weren't paying attention.

And, lately, I'd walked this forest many times at night with Lian, searching for Sabine's stash of moonshine. We'd race each other to climb to the top of a tree and then hang in the branches, imagining far-off worlds. Sometimes we imagined where Sabine was. Where she'd gone. Why she fled in the night just days after returning from a pilgrimage. What life she'd found out there that called her to leave us behind. Would I do the exact same thing? Would I find a life out there for me, better than this one? Would I never want to return? To live in Nimbaii, to become a healer? To a life with Lian?

Was that a life I even wanted? Did I want to marry Lian? We did spend every day together as it was—but was that the same as marriage? My stomach twisted.

How had I not noticed Lian's affections? How had I been so stupid? How had I not seen that he would drop other plans to spend time with me? That he always danced with me when I goaded him? And the way he would avert his eyes when I crawled out of the river, dripping wet, bare legs, as I raced for my towel?

And now, because I'd been so blind, I'd lost my best friend. And I had no idea what to say to make it better.

Perhaps there was nothing. It was my time for pilgrimage, after all. I was leaving for a whole year and, like Sabine, maybe I'd never come back. I couldn't commit to anything without knowing what else was in the galaxy.

I remembered the bonfire earlier that day, where Perse had told me it was better to start the pilgrimage sooner rather than later. The sooner I did it, the sooner I'd know what I wanted from my life. I never imagined I'd have secured a ship and a job the very same day. I wasn't clear on what this Evo company wanted with me. If I was consulting, they just wanted my opinion on something? But why did they specifically want a biokin?

I tried not to think if it could have been some kind of ruse. But I don't believe a whole tavern-worth of people would have volunteered to be a pilot if it were completely underhanded.

My chest felt tight, but I knew some things you couldn't plan for until you had more information. Tomorrow, I resolved, I would ask Mila about this Evo company. If she had an errand on the spacestation, surely, she could tell me more about Evo.

Hopefully, there were more questions Mila could answer. Like what kind of errand would she have on a spacestation that she didn't already have permission to board?

As I reached the edge of my village, I could smell the bonfire smoke still in the air from the party earlier. I stood for a minute, trying to soak in everything. Homes were scattered across the landscape, with branches tucked and woven back into their walls at they grew from saplings into homes. There were a few muted lights in the windows. The schoolhouse was the largest building in town, creating a silhouette against the forest. A few people sat at the bonfire, staring into the coals, soaking in their warmth. Would this be the last time I saw Nimbaii in my whole life?

I headed towards the fire to warm up one last time before heading in to bed. But as I got closer, I realised it was Lian sitting by the fire edge, speaking with his father. Lian threw some small twigs into the fire, shoulders drooping. I hesitated, not sure if I should interrupt. I didn't want to make things worse. Then, as I stepped back to retreat, a twig beneath my foot snapped. They both turned, startled. Lian stood up, eyes wide and took a half-step towards me. My breath caught in my throat. All the well thought out, reasonable discussions I'd planned in my head evaporated. "I'm leaving tomorrow," I said and turned and fled.

***

In the end, I didn't pack much. Realistically, if I landed on a planet with a different climate, I would need to buy clothes there. So, I folded a few spare dresses and undergarments in my backpack. I placed Perse's seeds in my medicine bag and laid my journal in my bag. I squeezed in the navcomm on top and pulled the drawstring closed. Finally, I tied Lian's bracelet around my wrist. My stomach felt hollow as I did it because I hadn't had the courage to say a real goodbye to him.

As I stepped out from the Nimbaii forest onto the paved streets of Tevinter, my palms started to sweat. I would be on a new planet in just a few days. I would be surrounded by a whole new universe: people speaking a language I didn't understand, wearing strange clothing, eating food I hadn't known existed. My heart hammered with excitement or fear. Perhaps both.

The distance to the spaceport felt endless as I walked in the blistering sun through the outskirts of Tevinter. I walked past *The Thirsty Captain*, which was silent and shut up in the daytime. I gave the building a nod, thanking it for finding my ride off-world. This time of day, there were few others on the street, only a few automated taxicabs zipped by me. I smiled, thinking that now I had credits that I could take a taxicab somewhere... once I worked out how to summon one.

I'd been to the Tevinter city centre several times on school excursions. We'd been to the art gallery on several occasions, looking at art not just from Tevinter but from other planets too. The paintings were captivating. Even more than the art, I loved being in the city. I would sit with Sabine and Lian outside the large sandstone art gallery, watching people. It was like a glimpse of being on another planet. People were everywhere, talking in different languages, sharing food I'd never seen. Children ran about laughing, playing games on the street. Parents argued. Teenagers danced on the road. People had skin, hair and clothing of all different colours and cuts. Despite this, children sometimes couldn't resist staring at our wool-spun outfits until an adult told them it was rude to stare.

However, this part of Tevinter was not anywhere near as beautiful as the refined city centre. I passed buildings that were drab cement blocks that sold spare parts for machinery or were storage houses for products, with taxicabs zipping in and out. Ahead, a street sign showed the city centre was left and the spaceport to the right, with a white moon symbol. Every time we'd passed that sign on a class excursion, Sabine had said, "We're one day closer to freedom." I supposed I shouldn't have been shocked that she'd left. Even when Nimbaii was all she knew, Sabine had always wanted something else. She would jump off the highest waterfalls and climb the tallest trees: Sabine always wanted adventure. I had just never thought she'd sneak out like a thief in the night.

I could hear the spaceport before I saw it: the sound of ships launching was deafening as they shot into the sky. I stood, mouth agape, watching the ships disappear in the clouds above. I had to pinch myself. I would soon be in space. When I finally turned a corner, there was the spaceport. It was a large building, bigger than the art gallery, but made of metal and glass. Taxicabs gathered around the entrance, people climbed in and out, and men loaded crates into larger taxivans. I covered my ears against the sounds of more ships launching. As I crossed the road to approach the spaceport, I dodged people with large bags, small dogs on leashes and children dashing about.

Glass doors slid open on their own and I stepped into the spaceport. I stared mouth agape for almost a minute at the building's interior. It was huge. Hundreds of people rushed by with bags. Automated carts zipped about on the shiny white floor, shops were selling bright clothing for different climates, and the smell of coffee made my stomach grumble. Signs overhead listed flights to different planets–I only recognised the planets that were home to other biokin. As I watched, the signs rotated to translate into languages I didn't recognise. I noticed a holoadvertising against the far wall, with a picture of a woman lying by a pool, wearing red lipstick and holding an orange drink. The starship in the background of the image looked bigger than the largest building I'd ever seen. "Travel the stars in opulence. Stardust cruises–now booking." Nearby was another holoscreen with a smiling man planting a sapling in red, desert-like soil. The caption read: "Evo | Greening galaxies." *Huh*. I would ask Mila about that later.

Someone shoved past me, absurdly high shoes clicking against the tiles as they rushed by. It was almost midday. I needed to find Mila somehow in this crowd and fast. *Ancients help me.* I scanned the room, trying to spot someone who looked like Mila. What if I couldn't find her in time? What if she left without me? *Cripes, what a start to my journey!* I turned to my right and saw a bank of machines printing out tickets for people. At the final machine, I recognised a familiar girl in a blue jumpsuit kicking its side. "Freaking heck, just give me my docking pass!"

The machine said in a robotic voice, "Please restate the request."

"I've paid my docking fee; now release my ship!" Mila growled.

"Please restate your request," the machine repeated.

Mila glowered. "*I want to talk to a human!*"

Someone nearby gave her a dirty look, and Mila responded, "Oh, shove off. It's just a ticket machine; it's not sentient."

The person held her gaze until she stabbed her finger at a sticker on the machine, which had a heart symbol with a cross through it.

"See?" she looked as if she was about to kick the bystander, too. The passerby peered at the sticker and then, mouth pursed, kept walking.

My fingers clasped Lian's bracelet, twisting it in my fingers. It seemed like Mila was having trouble getting her ship. What if Mila

couldn't get me to the Evo spacestation? What if her ship was im-
pounded? Or broken...?

The video screen switched over to a picture of a human woman
with bright orange lipstick, who asked Mila, "Can I help you?"

"Yeah. I paid my docking fee, and this broken machine hasn't released my ship."

"What's your ship?"

"The *Scout*."

"Identification?"

Mila pressed her thumb against a blinking red panel on the machine. Nothing happened for a long time, and Mila's foot tapped
impatiently. Then, finally, the panel switched to green, and the person
on the screen said, "Your ship is now released. Sorry for the delay. And
we'll get a tech to review the ticket machine."

"Thanks," Mila said, grabbing the tickets which were printed from
the machine. She shoved them into the pocket of her jumpsuit.

She spun around and took a step toward me, almost sending me
sprawling.

"Oh," she said, surprised to find me right there, "You weren't hard
to find."

"You aren't easy to miss," I shot back.

She paused for half a beat to take this in but then turned her attention to business. "Takeoff is in fifteen minutes," she started walking
across the spaceport without even checking if I was following. I darted
after her, dodging people with carts piled with suitcases taller than
them. Finally, we headed to the back of the spaceport and entered a
wide, beige hallway that led us away from the shops and crowds.

"This is the access to the private docking," she scanned the tickets
against a double set of doors, right as a cart barreled through the doors

with a crate full of goats. But then, she corrected herself, "And freight docking."

The hallway was far less glamorous than the other parts of the spaceport: the floor was a grey linoleum, and the lights were a harsh and hurt my eyes. It wasn't designed to impress anyone.

Mila kept walking down the hallway at speed, squeezing past autocarts hauling baggage. I jogged to keep up. We passed a long row of numbered doors; B2, B3, B4. She kept marching until, double-checking her printed ticket, we stopped at B12. There, she heaved open the heavy double door, and sunlight poured in. We stepped down onto the tarmac, where there were five small ships docked. On the other side of the spaceport sat white and silver ships larger than the whole spaceport itself–the cruise ships.

"Here we are," Mila said, pointing to a tiny ship at the back that, in my opinion, did not look spaceworthy. It had patches of metal welded to the outside, which looked like they'd been taken from several more impressive ships. The whole ship was not much larger than my cottage at home. Hand-painted in cursive on the side was the name, *Scout*.

She pulled a lever on the outside of the ship. A set of stairs lowered, and the door to the ship opened. She clambered in, and a moment later, the ship's engines begin to warm up, whirring noisily.

I exhaled to steady myself. This moment, right now, was the start of my pilgrimage. I was heading off into space with a girl who carried a knife in a spaceship that looked barely like it could fly. I was tasked with a mysterious job that only a biokin could help with. I didn't understand where I was going, and I wasn't even sure why Mila had agreed to take me. But I knew this was the first step of my journey–and the last time I would set foot on this planet in a very long time.

"Takeoff is in seven minutes," Mila said, leaning out from the ship's doorway. I grabbed the railing of the stairs and hauled myself in.

Four

Mila shut the main door and then manually cranked a handle, which closed a second thin door. A small panel on the wall lit up with a green light. The panel said we were airtight.

"I'll store your bag," she said, "while you strap in." She grabbed my backpack and headed somewhere in the back of the ship. There were only two seats at the front of the *Scout*, so I gathered this was where I was meant to sit. There was a dashboard with a hundred dials blinking like fireflies in summer. There was also a tiny vidscreen, which was blank except for the words *Tevinter Surface*.

What I suspected was the pilot's seat had been cobbled together from somewhere else, much like the rest of the ship. It was red and gold-lined and looked like it had been salvaged off a vessel owned by a wealthy merchant or a King of some distant planet. My seat, however, was a hard plastic material, but I hoped I wouldn't need to be sitting in it for long.

Mila climbed into the seat beside me and handed me a headset. She pulled her headset on, and I copied what she did.

"Testing, 1, 2."

I jumped as her voice was right in my ear, even over the roar of the engine.

"Yes, I can hear you."

"Roger."

She strapped a harness over her body and fastened the buckles. I found the clips on my seat and attempted to do the same, which, admittedly, took a considerable amount longer than her well-practised actions. The clasps fit together in a strange configuration, and it took a few attempts.

"*Scout* checking in. We're in preflight," she announced into her headset. I jumped again because a voice responded, "Roger. You will have flight path clearance in five,"

"Roger that."

"Who is Roger?"

"It's flight control," Mila gestured out the ship to a tower across the tarmac, as if that explained everything. She must fly a lot if she knew the name of the flight controller.

Mila glanced at each of the levers on the dashboard in turn, checking one thing or another and occasionally tweaking dials here and there. Her hands moved across the dashboard with ease, as if playing the flute.

"This is your first time heading out?" Mila asked, and I realised she was talking to me, not Roger.

"Yes," I called out, a little too loudly, forgetting the microphone on the headset wouldn't need me to yell.

"You might be a little uncomfortable during launch," she said. "But the queasiness will pass when we get out of atmo."

I nodded and then remembered the headset needed me to speak, I replied, "Okay." I didn't know what atmo was, but I was about to find out. I bit my lip as I thought about all the welded patches on the outside. Was this ship even spaceworthy? It was far too late to back out, and I reminded myself, this was part of my pilgrimage and part of becoming an adult. I took slow, deep breaths to calm myself.

Roger announced in my ear, "Flightpath is yours."

Mila peered at my buckle to ensure I was strapped in, and satisfied, held her hand over a thick black lever on the dashboard.

"Next stop: orbit," she said with a wild grin. It was the first time I'd seen her smile. "Launching in three–two–one–" and she pushed the lever to the top of the dashboard. The noise of the engine was deafening. It felt like being under a waterfall.

The ship lurched upward and bolted into the sky. It was like someone had punched me in the gut. All at once, the spaceport was no longer in view; it was just sky. We were racing towards the clouds far above us.

Hecking heck! I swore to myself as I was pinned down to my seat. My entire body was shaking, down to my eyelids.

I gripped the handles of the seat even tighter, my nails digging into the plastic arms as the vibrating of the *Scout* grew stronger. My mind raced. What if one of those welded on panels just tore right off? I shut my eyes for a second but thought I would hurl, so I opened them again to focus on the massive cloud we were racing towards.

Ancient ones, keep me safe, I prayed as we shot into the sky.

As we met the clouds, they exploded into water droplets around us. Moments later, the water droplets had slid from the windscreen, and the sky changed colour. The sky shifted from light blue to a dazzling orange sunset, then finally to a deep ocean blue. Then, in another instant, the sky was pitch black, dotted with stars glistening like river sand in the sun. The shaking smoothed out as we staggered into actual space.

My breath caught at the beauty of the black and star-studded sky rolling out ahead of us. I could see bright red and blue planets blinking across the sky, swirling constellations and shooting stars. Space. We were in space. None of the campfire stories from Perse or Mum or Dad or Sabine could describe this.

Mila pulled the lever down, and the ship stopped shaking, the roaring engine cut down to a quiet hum. It was like we were coasting along a lazy river.

"You okay?" Mila called, eyes bright and cheeks flushed.

"Yes!" I stammered, gasping for air.

Mila double-checked the dashboard, entered into the vid screen *'Evo space station–Tevinter'*. She entered some more items into the vidscreen, and we settled into space. As the ship's direction shifted, I could see my blue planet curved below us.

I once thought the art gallery in Tevinter City was the largest thing in the world, something I bet Sabine would have laughed at, so I never said it out loud. But now, the whole city was smaller than my littlest finger. And the forest, where I'd spent a lifetime running in the forest, swimming in the river, skimming rocks with Lian, cooking eggplant stew with my Dad and playing Mic-Mac with my Mum, was just a speck against the planet.

My mouth was dry.

"I'm going to be sick," I gasped.

Mila unstrapped herself from her seat and pulled out a paper bag from somewhere under the dashboard. Hands shaking, I ripped off my headset and vomited ungraciously into the bag for a few minutes.

"You good?" Mila asked. Pale and sweaty, I nodded.

"We're on auto for a couple of hours," she said, pointing to the navconsole. "Let me show you around."

My stomach still gurgled, and Mila handed me a pouch of water which I sipped tentatively.

After a minute, I could stand and take in the *Scout* for the first time. My first impression that it wasn't bigger than my home in Nimbaii, mostly the room we were in. The ship smelled metallic and faintly of mushrooms. The ship hummed quietly, partly the engines, partly the air piping in through the vents about the ship.

"This is the pilot bay," she said, pointing to the two chairs at the front. Then, she turned the chairs around, facing the centre of the *Scout* and waved a hand to show the newly configured space, "This is the rec room." I wasn't sure if that was meant to be funny.

She strode across the room and pointed out a set of cabinets that, once unfolded, turned into a small kitchenette. "Galley," she announced, and pulling down a table from a cabinet, she set it into the floor by the two chairs she unfolded from a wall. "Dining room."

"So... versatile."

Hidden behind the galley was a cubicle only slightly larger than me, which held both a shower and a toilet. Mila showed me how it switched between the two with the clunky pull of a lever on the outside. "It's a work in progress," Mila muttered.

Behind us were the sleeping quarters, discreetly tucked behind unremarkable metallic doors. On the left was a doorway to Mila's quarters, and on the right were my quarters. My room was a small, sparse space that barely had room for a bed. It was nothing like my room at home which smelled of vanilla and was piled with books, blankets, plants and, I confess, a light scattering of my clothes all over the floor. Here, the only thing on the walls were the dented metallic cabinets where Mila had already placed my backpack. It was bare otherwise. I knew Mila didn't usually have passengers, so I shouldn't have been surprised by the spartan nature of the room, but when she briefly opened the door to her room, hers looked just as bare. I could see a pile of ship manuals strapped into a shelf on the wall and above her bed was taped a photo of what looked like her family. She quickly shut the door before I could get a closer look.

"Always put your things away in the locker," she said, "You don't want things flying about as we travel and knocking one of us unconscious."

"Okay."

She nodded to a hatch in the floor at the back of the room. It revealed a ladder to somewhere beneath us.

"This is engineering," she pointed. "The only time you're allowed in there is if I'm dead." I don't think that was a joke. "And that's the tour."

"Thank you again," I said, "For taking me off-world. I can't think of what I'd have done otherwise." I thought of the burly man from the tavern and shuddered.

"It's no problem," she shrugged, "It's an easy trip for me, and I get paid,"

"So, is that what you do? To get credits? Transport people?"

"Not people. Things."

"I'm not a thing."

"You're a one-time job."

"Because you have an errand to run on Evo?"

"Generally, I do odd jobs. Transport things. Help people out with favours." I noticed she didn't answer my question.

"I never knew women could own spaceships," I blurted out like a child.

"Not everyone wants to live out in space."

"But you're okay with it? Living alone here?"

"I like having a roof over my head," she said, patting the hatch of the ship like it was a dog. "But *Scout* and I have been through a lot together, so I wouldn't want it any other way."

"Doesn't your family miss you?" I asked, thinking of the photo.

Her lips drew tight. "I don't know."

I shifted uncomfortably from one foot to another.

Mila tucked a curl that had fallen loose from her ponytail behind her ear. "Well," she said, "I need to check on the levels," and she started climbing down the hatch to engineering.

"Wait," I called out to her. "How long till we reach this Evo spacestation?"

"Three hours."

"And... what does this Evo company do?"

"You'd never heard of Evo? They're the largest agribusiness in the galaxy," she said. "If you eat something, they probably made it. Or a part of it. Or owned the land it was grown on."

"Oh," I said. Mila climbed down the hatch and shut it loudly, leaving me alone.

I looked about the tiny spaceship. It hummed quietly as we headed towards this spacestation. I pinched myself. I was breathing recycled air and my feet were just inches from space. I'd spent my life breathing air filled with the thick scent of pine, and my feet covered in dirt. The only time I saw the stars was at nighttime by the bonfire as Dad would point out the constellations and share stories from the time of Ancient Ones.

I wandered back towards the pilot bay and spun the co-pilot seat around to face towards space. I sat, soaking in the stars. Space was absolutely breathtaking.

Being surrounded by the night sky was like the time Sabine dared me to swim to the bottom of the waterfall. There were so many shades of black and blue that rippled around me. The distant galaxies were so colourful. I wondered what those planets would be like. Was the air of those far-off planets red and orange like the constellations made them look from here? Now I would *find out*.

I tried to spot this spacestation we were headed to out the window, but I could only see the inky sky. What did Evo want with me? I know that biokin had powers to connect with plants that other humans didn't have, but I still didn't know how I could 'consult for them'. I tugged at Lian's bracelet on my wrist. Was I walking into something dangerous? They did put a bounty on finding a biokin from the Nimbaii forest, which did seem a strange way to contract someone for work.

It would just be a few hours consulting, I told myself, and then I would be off to the next planet Mila was headed to; she'd drop me off, and I'd begin my pilgrimage for real. I bit my lip to hold back a little squeal of excitement. I was here, doing it.

Back in my quarters I crawled into my bunk, intending to journal. But I had barely slept the night before, so I fell asleep on top of the covers, fully dressed. The gentle hum of the ships' engines reminded me of a waterfall in winter, and before I knew it, I was sleeping.

***

Mila rapped on the metal door, waking me.

"Arriving at the station in thirty," Mila announced. I groggily sat up, momentarily having forgotten where I was.

"If you were going to wash, now is a good time," she said, passing a towel from an overhead locker. Mila had showered and changed into a new jumpsuit with a dark blue, almost purple colour. She wore a green tank top underneath, and she'd twisted her hair into a knot on top of her head. She looked a lot less like the impulsive girl who had pulled a knife on a man in a bar and, well, I supposed, a professional pilot.

I went to the bathroom and undressed in the tiny cubicle. There was a transparent cube in the wall, where I placed my clothing so it wouldn't get wet when I turned on the shower. I put my towel and garments in there and turned the knobs on the wall. The shower cubicle didn't pour out water like the showers back home, but instead, a fine mist burst from all sides of the stall. I didn't feel refreshed like the warm shower at home, but I did feel clean. I quickly scrubbed myself down with soap and turned off the mist shower. I pulled on my nicest bluebell cotton dress. I pulled my hair back into a ponytail and inspected my face in the mirror. I still looked tired, but I hoped, presentable.

I headed back to my bunk, stowed away my backpack in the locker, and exhaled. Was I ready? As ready as I was ever going to be for entering the unknown.

I headed out to the pilot bay and strapped in to the seat. When I looked out of the window, the sky was a blanket of stars and glowing planets around us. When I finally spotted the Evo spacestation, I had initially taken it for a moon. It looked much bigger than one of those cruise spaceships I'd seen. It had large metal spheres bulging out of it, like giant bubbles. I wondered how many years it had taken to build something that size. I stopped breathing for a full minute.

Mila climbed into the pilot seat and took a long slow breath out. I wondered what she had to be nervous about.

She switched the ship control from auto to manual mode, and she tightly gripped a steering column. Our ship slowed to half the speed as we got close to the station. The station loomed around us, and it was so large that it blocked the stars beyond it. The outside of the spacestation was covered in writing of different dock numbers, and metal pipes spidered their way over the entire structure. Mila looked as if she was concentrating on ensuring she didn't crash the *Scout* right into the spacestation—which, I suspected, she probably was. Through her headset, she was communicating with someone on the radio, also apparently named Roger. He directed us to docking bay 14, which

Mila navigated to at a snail's pace. When the voice said, "Docking secured", she looked visibly relieved.

We unstrapped ourselves from our seats and headed over to the main exit. Mila pressed a button, an external door whirred open, but our internal airlock door was still closed. Her hand hovered over the crank to pull the door open.

"Are you ready?" she asked.

How could I ever be ready for my first visit to a spacestation? Or to, for that matter, a visit to the largest agribusiness in the galaxy? "Sure."

She started to wind the crank for the inner door but turned to me, biting her lip. She looked at me in a way I'd never seen before. Like she was telling me a secret. "Look–I don't know why Evo wants you, but..." she hesitated. "You know you don't need to give them everything, right?"

"Okay," I said. What was I walking into?

She smiled a grim, tight smile and cranked open the door release.

Air hissed into the *Scout* as it met the oxygen from the Evo spacestation. My heart was racing, and time felt like it slowed down, as I stepped into the bright white tunnel.

Five

As we stepped off the *Scout*, I realised we were in a long white corridor that looked like it was made of plastic tubing. When we reached the end of the tube, we reached a glass wall. On the other side was a room that looked larger than the whole schoolhouse at Nimbaii. It was a reception lobby with comfortable looking green couches, and all the tables were white and circular. A woman in a neat black jumpsuit and a pair of those strange high shoes I'd seen at Tevinter spacestation stood there, waiting. She had peroxide blonde hair, which contrasted against her dark skin, and thin eyes hidden behind large glasses. She was subtly shifting her weight onto her left foot, then right, then left again, eyes darting about.

I approached the glass doors, waiting for them to open like they had at the spaceport. Instead, the woman just stood, watching us, waiting for something. Then, behind us, a glass door closed, and I yelped, realising we were now trapped in a glass cube. *What was happening?* My heart started to race.

I turned to Mila, who softly murmured, "Standard decontamination process." The only sounds were the hum of oxygen being piped in. The room smelled sickeningly sweet. I twisted my fingers together. A soothing robot voice said, "Contamination assessment." What would happen if we didn't meet the test? I had no idea. Would we be told to leave the ship? Or would we be thrown in captivity? Or worse, would one of those machines piping in air change a mysterious setting and become something that turned us into a crispy meatball? Mila tapped her navcomm against her waist. The automated voice repeated, "Contamination assessment." Finally, after a long few seconds, the voice announced, "Clear." I realised I'd been holding my breath and inhaled sharply. The glass doors at the front of the cube sprang open.

We stepped into the bright lobby. The white-blonde haired woman breathed as if in a hurry, "Hello and welcome to the Tevinter Evo station. My name is Rebecca. How may I direct you?"

Mila lifted her chin and said in a crisp, business-like voice that I'd never heard before, "I'm Mila Riley. I'm here with the delivery of the biokin from Tevinter."

"Wonderful," said Rebecca, with a smile that didn't meet her eyes. "Deliveries are down this way." She led us to the white reception desk. I now noticed that the wall behind the desk had a mosaic made of live plants, spelling the word Evo. Paper lantern lights hung from the roof. *Paper*, I thought. *Expensive.*

Rebecca accessed a vidscreen on her desk and spoke to someone on her headset. "Hello, Mr. Vulant. You've got a delivery from Tevinter. Mila Riley. Uh-huh. Yes. Perfect."

I noted that everyone seemed to call me a *delivery* and not a *guest*. I tried not to think about Mila's warning.

We waited for this Mr. Vulant to arrive, but he took his time. We ended up sitting on the couches at Rebecca's invitation. I bet I'd counted every single tile on the floor when Mr. Vulant entered the lobby from a side door.

When he stepped into the room, Rebecca stood a little taller and stammered, "Mr. Vulant!"

Mr. Vulant was a large man who seemed to take up more space than his actual height just by the way he stood–feet apart, back straight.

He wore a charcoal-coloured jumpsuit and had metal ornaments sewn into his shoulders. He had an Evo badge at his waist and the shiniest black shoes I had ever seen. He had greying hair at his temples and a small mouth.

"Ms. Riley," he held out his hand to shake, and Mila glided over to him. Mila held her shoulders back in an unnatural way to make her look more confident. They looked to be caught in a power game I didn't understand. As she shook his hand, she looked him directly in the eyes for a long time.

"Mila Riley," she said finally, "Delivering the biokin."

"Richard Vulant," he replied, "Head of Innovation here at Evo. I hope it wasn't too much trouble to come here?"

"Not at all." Everyone seemed to ignore the fact that she didn't come here out of the generosity of her own heart; she was being *paid*. Of course, it wasn't *trouble* to come here.

I hesitantly stepped over towards them. "I'm Addison Nora," I said since no one seemed to be introducing me.

Richard's eyes landed on me, and taking me in, smiled artificially like Rebecca did. "Our biokin! Thank you for your time. We're so grateful for your help."

"No problem," I replied, my voice flat. This man, and this place, and the way people artificially spoke felt off. It was so unlike Nimbaii.

"Ms. Riley," Richard turned to Mila, "You're welcome to wait here if you like?"

"No," Mila and I said together at once. I didn't want to be left alone here. I was surprised that Mila had responded that she wanted to come too, but I imagined she had her own reasons. Her own *secret* reasons.

"Fair enough," Richard gestured to the room he'd come from. "This way."

He put his Evo badge against a white box next to the door, and the door slid open for him. We followed him down a long hallway.

There was glass set into the walls along the corridor. In the rooms on either side of us, people were working in laboratories, with computers all over the walls. They wore lab coats, gloves and sometimes even complete suits with facemasks. Chemicals, glass tanks, ferns, flowers and sun lamps were over the benches. It was strange to see plants in this artificial environment, so far from home. I spotted a stunning yellow and white flower in a glass tank, all alone in a vial of water. I imagined it's homeworld, a lush rainforest, with trees that reached the sky, and giant red beetles clamouring to feast on scattered berries. This place seemed so sterile. How could you study plants away from nature? The people in the lab kept focused on their work, inspecting items under microscopes, putting plants in machines, writing notes down on their research.

Mila looked like she was scanning every single room intently, like searching for something. She kept pace right behind Mr. Vulant, answering small talk about her voyage here without pausing a beat.

Turning to me, Richard asked, "So, you're a biokin."

"Yes."

"We are very interested to see what you can do."

"Um. Happy to help. What is it that a Head Of Innovation does?" I asked, hoping for a little small talk of my own.

"I fix problems other people have created," he said, his mouth becoming tight, and I thought that was more to himself than to me.

After walking for a couple of minutes, we paused at a new door, at which Richard again used his Evo badge against the wall panel to open the doors.

We entered a large room with a dark carpet, a set of long desks and a series of vidscreens built into the walls. The vidscreens looked like they had images that were the surface of many different planets. There was a forest. A desert. And icy tundra vista. I wondered what planets they were.

I turned and saw that at a desk was a woman in a lab coat. She wore a red turtleneck sweater and tight orange pants, with a long Evo lanyard hanging around her neck. Even though she was sitting down, she was really, really tall. She was typing something on a vidscreen, and as Richard entered, she stood to greet us.

"Mr. Vulant–I'm just finishing up here–" she said quickly, and she began typing faster.

"No problem at all, Eefah," he said. "We'll head straight in."

"Yes, I'm finished in there," she said, waving in the general direction of another door.

Richard turned to enter a code in the keypad. He pressed his thumb to a touchpad but, remembering Mila, turned with an apologetic pout, "I'm sorry, Ms. Riley. Going past this point is for biokin only. You will need to wait here." He gestured to a grey couch nearby.

Mila shrugged nonchalantly, settling into the couch expansively. "I can entertain myself," she said coolly. She dropped her gaze to the woman across from her, who blushed ever so slightly.

"How long exactly will we take?" I asked.

"We shouldn't be more than a couple of hours."

What could I be "helping out" with that could take so little time and be worth a thousand credits? I didn't want Mila to leave me alone here, but her gaze was solidly fixed on Eefah, and she didn't seem inclined to move. I took in a slow, deep breath. *Okay,* I thought. *Let's get this over with.*

Richard entered the pin code into the door next to him. The door swung open. I heard Mila turn to Eefah and ask in a silky voice, "Sorry, excuse me—I can see you're very busy—but I'm absolutely dying for a coffee, do you know—" and the door shut behind me.

I stepped through the doorway, and we were in another hallway. This one reminded me of the freight hallway we'd passed at the space-port: it was thin and grey and looked entirely for efficiency.

We passed some numbered doors, and finally, we stepped through a new doorway.

And that was when my mouth dropped open.

We hadn't stepped into a room. Instead, we'd stepped into a planet.

Six

I looked about in awe: we were in a savannah. Across the grassland were short, squat trees and mountains. The grass was up to my knees, and the heat was hot and dry. Bugs started darting about me. I turned behind me to understand how I'd stepped onto a planet, but realised the wall behind me was painted. If the door was closed, it would have been almost invisible from this side.

"*Where are we?*"

Richard smiled, showing all his teeth. It was clear he loved watching people enter this room in awe.

"This is one of our research biodomes. We've replicated the environments of several planets so we can examine how our plants grow in those places."

"I don't understand." Wouldn't you just grow plants in their native environments?

"We make these spaces like their native habitats, but with a few changes to test how our plants react." Seeing my blank expression, he continued, "At Evo, we make it easy for communities to settle on new worlds. We help develop plants that can grow in unique environments." His voice changed to a sing-song tilt, which made me think this next part was something he'd recited many, many times. "Let's say a family wants to settle on a new planet, but it's a scorching desert. They might want to plant some rheno to eat, and we all know rheno cannot survive the heat. So, we will develop a new kind of rheno for them, splicing some attributes of desert plants that can survive in the heat. That means the new rheno will survive even in extremely high temperatures, and the new colonists can eat."

"Oh," I said, surprised. I knew you could grow one cutting off another, but not that you could take individual attributes of one plant and give them to another. Considering we'd just passed about a dozen science labs, I guessed they used very advanced technology to do it.

"We save lives," Richard said, in a grandiose way, "We help people who would starve to death otherwise. It's why we're so grateful to have your help."

I couldn't help flushing at this.

"So," Richard continued, "I wanted to explain what we do to give you some background on this project we want your help with. We understand that biokin can communicate with plants?"

"We can connect with them," I say, "So we can find them in the forest."

Richard's eyes light up as if I was a child who had given the correct answer in a schoolroom. "You can find plants? Perfect–that's exactly what we need your help with!"

He held up a finger, indicating I needed to wait as he pulled a little tablet device from under his arm and handed it to me. "But first–we've got some paperwork."

I looked at the tablet, and I could read the words on the screen, but the sentences were so complex, I couldn't work out what they meant. "Just put your thumbprint at the bottom. It's a standard contract."

I didn't understand what he was asking me to agree to, but as I placed my thumb on the bottom of the device, it gave a slight pinch, and a bead of my blood retracted into the machine.

"Now the formalities are over, let's begin," he began walking further into the savannah and I followed.

As we walked further into the hot sun–well, it felt like sun, but I supposed it was all artificial lights–we walked past some metal rods in the ground with lights on the end. I realised they were laid out in a series of circles in the grass. After a few minutes, we stopped in the centre.

"First thing we need to do is confirm that you can link with plants," he said.

"I can connect with plants," I said, a little hotly.

"It's all just standard procedure," he reassured me. "We have scientists who are monitoring your progress," he pointed to the metal rods in the ground. I spotted for the first time a small metal device that was flying nearby. My stomach twisted.

"Please sit," he indicated the savannah floor, "And I'd like you to connect with these plants as far as you can," he said. "These lights will show us how far you can reach."

I sat down in the grass. This was seriously what Evo brought me here for? No, he said something about finding a plant. I forced myself to ignore the clenching at the top of my stomach and closed my eyes. I exhaled slowly and began the process of connecting with the savannah. My body pressed against the ground, my feet tucked under me and my hands fell into my lap. The scent of wild sage, dry grass and dust were on the breeze. I opened my awareness to the sounds of the biodome. Insects were buzzing, and grass rustled in the breeze. There was a crunching sound nearby which I imagined was Richard. The thought of him watching me intently made me lose my concentration briefly, but I focused again on my connection. The sweltering sun beat down on my back and head. And I tapped into the grass I sat amongst. In my vision, it lit up like fireflies. Each stalk lit up in a circle around me.

I pushed out my awareness, extending my reach further and further around the ring. As I passed by the metal rods, each left a tiny pinprick in my awareness as I touched each one.

I extended out to several of the rings. An irregular tapping sound caught my attention, and I realised it was Richard, jabbing notes into his tablet. The thought of him staring at me, measuring me, made my chest feel tight. Finally, my reach wavered, and I snapped out of the connection. As my eyes opened, the rods with lights around me were lit up as far as I'd reached with my awareness. Richard made a note on his device on how far I'd reached.

"Okay," Richard said. "That's a good reach."

He pointed to another area in the grassland, closer to the door we've entered from. He started walking towards it casually, and I followed suit.

"Now, the reason we have brought you here–" and he referred to some notes on his tablet–"is that we've lost a precious flower. As you can imagine, it can cost us a lot of money to design a flower that can survive in different environments. Unfortunately, it has been–misplaced–by some staff who are no longer with us. Can you help us find it?" He held out a photo of the small yellow and white flower. "I can try," I said and looked about the savannah. This place was huge. Even at my largest reach due to my adventures with Lian, it would take hours to search a grid to look in this entire biodome.

He pointed to the grass near us, and I sat cross-legged. I supposed we needed to start somewhere. There were more rods in the ground near us. I closed my eyes and focused on my weight, the sounds of insects buzzing, the sensations of warmth and cold on my body. I connected again with the grass. In my head, the grass lit up, and I pushed my awareness out, out, out. I wasn't sensing a flower. I could only feel the grass. Or some of those trees I'd seen in the distance. I extended my reach out further and further than I had last time. But no flower. I called to Richard, "I can't find a flower," I struggled to maintain my reach and push out to search even further, but nothing.

"Oh well," Richard said dryly, "Let's check the next biodome."

My eyes snapped open. It wasn't even *in here*? There was another biodome to check? How many biodomes did they have?

"I'm sorry?" I said, not hiding the irritation in my voice.

Richard shrugged, "It was released in a biodome; we need to check a few of them."

"But I haven't searched the whole space–" I objected.

"Never mind," he snapped. "We only need you to search *this* area."

I couldn't shake the feeling that something wasn't quite right about this task. I couldn't put my finger on it. What was it? I stood up, brushed the grass off my skirt angrily and followed Richard.

We exited the biodome, and we walked down the drab hallway. Richard opened the door to another biodome and indicated that I should enter. It was a drab mountaintop, and there was ice on the ground. My eyes widened as I looked at my thin cotton dress. I would freeze in there!

"Mr. Vulant!" a voice called out behind us.

"Taminda," he nodded towards her. A woman with pale skin jogged down the hallway to meet Richard. She was another scientist with a messy bun and tired eyes. As she approached, she held out a tablet for Richard to look at. He gestured for me to head inside the biodome while they spoke. I tentatively stepped inside, but an icy wind whipped at me. I wrapped my arms around myself in an attempt to stay warm. More of the metal rods surrounded this mountaintop, and I stepped towards the centre of the circle. The wind howled, and my teeth chattered already.

I jogged back to the hallway to ask Richard for a coat. They were facing the other direction, poring over the tablet, and the woman asked Richard, "Do you know if she is one?"

Richard shook his head, "We don't know yet. We haven't reached the final biodome yet,"

"Well, does she have the markers?"

"We're still processing her blood."

"Let me know when you know."

"I will," he said.

And I knew I had overheard something I shouldn't. My blood felt cold. The markers? *Oh, Ancients–what did that mean?!* I jogged into the centre of the circle of light rods. I stood there, shivering, pretending I'd been out of earshot during that conversation.

Were they doing tests to see if I had something called markers? We weren't even in the biodome where they were running the important test they needed. My stomach roiled. This was some kind of ruse. But I didn't understand what was going on. At all.

My cheeks burned. I had believed that story about the lost flower in these biodome, even though it was obviously a tropical flower that would need heat and humidity, and–I realised why it seemed off. *I'd seen the flower already.* We'd passed it in the lab on the way over. *It wasn't even lost.* They knew where it was. So, this was just some ruse to get me to connect to these biodomes. Why, Ancients, would they want to trick me into connecting with the biodomes?

My fingers and toes were now shaking. Mr. Vulant entered and gestured to the ground. "Let's get this over with,"

"The ground has ice on it!" I protested.

"And the sooner you connect, the sooner we can go!"

But the woman stared at me, eyes wide, "Richard–it's freezing in here. And we–we don't need to search here," she said, enunciating the last few words slowly.

I didn't need to be told twice. I jogged to the exit, giving Taminda a grateful look.

Richard's jaw clenched, but we moved to another biodome. There were coastal grasses and warm sun, at which my shoulders unclenched. I wondered in the back of my mind if this was the biodome they had discussed. The one that would tell them if I was what they were looking for. My gut twisted. I had a feeling I didn't want to be the one they were after.

I clambered through the sand dunes to the circle of light rods and sat in the warm sand.

I didn't like being lied to. Or used. And here was both–even though I didn't understand what was happening. But I had one secret on my side. They didn't know how far I could reach with my connection. And I was determined to do everything I could to work out what was going on.

I needed to calm down if I was going to be smart. But, luckily for me, meditation was exactly the way to do that. So, I shut my eyes and slowly exhaled. I was getting more used to meditating while being watched by Richard.

The sand beneath me was warm, and it crept into my socks and boots. The wild grasses about me stuck into my skin, and the warm sun beat down on me. The air was moist here and smelled like salt and seaweed. Sea birds were squawking, and waves lapped at a shore. I connected with thin grass around me. Now that I knew it was a ruse, I didn't bother searching for the flower; I just extended my reach as far as I could. I brushed by the grasses, the coastal trees, connecting further and further out. Finally, I reached the boundary of the light rods and pushed beyond them. I smiled to myself that I hadn't revealed how far my powers could reach. I could extend my mind much, much further than they knew.

In my time with Lian, I'd stretched across vast distances of the forest. Even Perse had been impressed. I pushed further along the coast. There was a dip on one edge of my awareness, and the plants shifted to seaweed and algae, so there must have been actual water here, not just sounds being played. On the other edge, I hit a wall of the biodome. I kept pushing further and further, trying to find out as much about this space as I could. And as I pushed, I realised there was a small crack in the wall through to the dome next to it. I squeezed my awareness through the gap and burst through to the other side, extending my reach to the biodome next to us. It was a warm forest, much like my forest back home. The feeling of trees calmed me, and I extended my connection to its limit. My reach wavered. Fueled by anger, I redirected my attention, pulling my awareness from the ocean and further into the forest, connecting to trees, saplings and vines. And then I connected with someone.

And I snapped out of my mediation. *What the heck?*

"Did you find the flower?" Richard asked, looking up from his tablet.

"Let me try again," I said, "I–I am still recovering from the cold."

My hands were now shaking. I poured all of my efforts into directing my reach through the tiny hole in the biodome through to the forest biodome next door.

And I connected with someone on the other side. But not someone. Not really. It's a tree. But one that felt different. Like it can think. And a shiver ran down my spine. *Is it an Ancient One?*

I didn't think Gods still existed. But here I was. Connecting to a tree that can connect with me.

In my mind's eye, an image flashed into my awareness. It was a picture of a large, gnarled tree, with hollows and roots so big a human could hide inside. Its bark was rough, its leaves thin. And I realised it's the tree, sending me an impression of itself.

I gasped, and I worked on visualising myself, sitting here, in the coastal grasses, and I sent the image back.

And, in return, I received a picture of birds in flight.

My stomach dropped. *Because I knew what this meant.*

All at once, I remembered a childhood game I played with Lian and Sabine. It was a game in our village that even Perse had played as a child. One person plays the eyeless monster, another person plays a traveler who cannot hear, and the third person is the navigator, who cannot speak. The traveler needs to travel through the monster's territory (usually Lian, with a blindfold), while the navigator could only communicate with the traveler using symbols with their hands. Each player takes one step at a time, trying to work their way across the field. Sabine would play the navigator, holding up symbols for *stop-move forward-step back*. And I would follow, putting my trust in her directions. And the signs were always what we had on hand. A rock. A stick. Or a feather. And to step back–to flee–was a bird's feather.

And all in a moment, I knew what this image meant. *It was asking for help.*

I paled. How could I help it? There was so much here I didn't understand; how could I assist a tree?! I was on a spacestation; it was my first time leaving my planet! I barely even understood where I was, let alone had any control over what I could do.

I sent back an impression of a leaf in a river, spiraling out of control. I wanted to show that I couldn't help it.

It responded with a picture of seeds high in its branches, scattering to the wind. *Children. It's looking for its children.* My palms started to sweat.

Again, I sent back the leaf tumbling in a river. *What does it expect me to do?*

It sent back a vision of a beanstalk wrapped about corn. The two plants grow stronger when the support of each is there for the other. We could help each other. My heart beat faster.

What does it want from me? What can I do?

And then it sent an image of a single spark. And then a flame. And it turned into fire. *Strength,* I think. And suddenly, my head was an explosion of fire. Someone sent a bolt of lightning into my brain, and my eyes burned. There was red everywhere. I was shivering and my stomach felt like it was trying to leap out of my mouth.

Suddenly the lightning bolt in my brain was over, but my eyes still thudded.

And finally, there was a single image. A rock. *Stay silent.*

I sent an image of rock back to show I understood, but I tore myself from the connection and ungraciously leaned over and vomited into the sand.

My eyes thudded, and my hands shook.

"What on earth --" I heard Richard exclaim.

Taminda shoved her tablet into his hands and exclaimed, "Of course she's sick! You had her in minus fifteen degrees! She's in shock!"

Weakly, I wiped my mouth, mind racing. Should tell them what happened? The tree had asked for silence. And, suddenly, I remembered Mila's words. *"You don't need to give them everything... Just be careful, okay?"* I wasn't sure if I should trust the tree, but I certainly didn't trust Richard. And the enemy of my enemy is my friend. *Okay, Ancient One, I'll help you.*

"Are we—are we done?" I asked.

Richard's eyes narrowed.

"No," he said stiffly, "We haven't found the flower."

Taminda leaned over me and gently rubbed my back. She sent daggers with her eyes to him, "Mr. Vulant—there's no need—"

"You don't have rank here," he snapped back. "This is an expensive exercise, and it's not complete yet."

Taminda held her mouth open to object but then closed it.

She stood and helped me up, "Let's get you some water first."

Seven

I leaned against the wall of the grey hallway, nursing my head, sipping the water. My hands were still shaking. What the heck happened? Did I meet an Ancient One? What was it doing here on the Evo spacestation? And why did it ask for help? And why did it give me a splitting headache?

"You okay?" asked Taminda.

"I'm feeling better," I said, clutching the glass. I was lying, of course. My head burned, but I didn't want Evo to know that they had a rogue tree on their ship talking to anyone strolling about the hallways. Well, any biokin, at least.

Richard looked at his watch pointedly. Then he walked down the hallway and opened another door into a new biodome.

"This is the final biodome," Taminda said softly.

I stood and walked into the final environment, and my legs felt weak. It was a forest. Through the trees, surrounded by the metal rods, was a large, gnarled tree. I knew it was the one I'd been speaking to. I remembered its final message: *silence.* And so, I pretended nothing was wrong. I stepped further into the biodome and walked through leaf litter and dirt. The forest smelled like home. I twisted my fingers through Lian's bracelet.

Richard nodded to the circle of rods, and I noticed they were placed right next to the Ancient One. And I realised that this tree is what they wanted me to connect with. This is the real reason they brought me here and put me through all these tests. But why? What would that tell them? How will this show if I am the one they are trying to find–whatever that means?

I sat in the leaf litter in the middle of the ring of rods, and I dug my fingers into the cool soil. It calmed me.

"Okay," said Richard, "One final place to search for the flower."

My hands were shaking. *What happens when I connect with the tree? Will I vomit again? Will they see that I'm the one they are looking for?* I pursed my lips and close my eyes.

I felt my body against the leaf litter. I heard bird calls around me. I could smell the earthy forest floor. And I linked with the forest. First, to the tiny saplings and the trees close to me. I extended out my reach further, but I hovered just this side of the tree, not daring to touch it.

"Further," Richard murmurs, "I've seen you go further in the first test."

My reach wavered as he interrupted me, but knowing I had no choice, I pushed my link out to envelop the Ancient Tree. I braced myself for the connection.

But nothing happened.

Silence.

I exhaled; grateful I didn't start vomiting again.

I kept extending my reach, hoping that it would satisfy Richard, and he'd let me go sooner. And then, on the far side of the tree, I connected with a tiny white and yellow flower.

I smiled, and I snapped my eyes open.

"The flower is beyond that tree," I said, pointing.

Richard was silent for a while, watching my expression. I keep calm. I didn't want him to think there was anything odd with this biodome.

"Do you want me to go and get it?" I asked, standing.

"No," said Richard, lips pursed. "We're done here."

I stood and started walking towards the exit.

He turned to Taminda and asked softly, "What do you think?"

"She had no reaction," she confirmed.

"Let's see if the blood test shows anything," he murmured.

My heart began to race. Would Evo know if I connected to the Ancient Tree from my blood? My head started swimming again. I needed to get out of here as soon as I could.

"Can I go now?"

Taminda nodded, but Richard shook his head. Taminda raised an eyebrow and hissed, "You saw she had no reaction. And she's still in shock from the mountain. Let's call it. We can get her back if the blood shows anything odd." She casually looked at her navcomm, "Besides, don't you have a meeting now?"

Richard looked at his own watch, lips pursing, and he gave a single short, sharp nod.

He led me back to the office that Mila had been waiting in. Mila had become close friends with the scientist from the lab during that time. Sitting casually on a desk, leaning close to the woman, she was murmuring, "Uh-huh. I'm in this sector all the time. Next time I'm here, I'll-"

She slid off the desk when she saw us re-enter, stepping an entire foot back from the scientist.

"Finished already?" Mila asked, a half-smile on her lips.

This wasn't like the Mila I'd met on the ship. She turned the charm on and off when it suited her. I wondered if getting back on a ship with her was just as dangerous as being here with Evo. Especially since I didn't know anything about her. But, remembering her warning, she seemed like she was on my side. Or, at least, not Evo's side? *The enemy of my enemy.*

Richard strode in, handing the tablet to Eefah. "Thank you, Mila, your biokin has been very helpful," he said, in a clipped tone of voice that sounded like I was not helpful at all.

"She was a little space sick," Taminda mentioned. My face flushed.

"Again?" Mila asked, and I shrugged. She turned to Richard, "I believe you owe me my credits?"

"Give your details to Rebecca at the front desk, and she'll process your payment." he said, "We pay quarterly."

Mila paused, "You won't pay me for *three months*?"

Richard nodded, "Yes, standard payment terms for our accounts department."

"No problem," said Mila through gritted teeth.

Richard led us through to the lobby, where Mila diligently gave Rebecca her details for payment to her navcomm–twice–so there was no mistake with the digits. Mila then showed me how to do the same. Then we were back on the *Scout*.

As soon as the *Scout*'s doors were closed and Mila had cranked the airtight seal, Mila dropped her perky demeanour and looked exhausted.

"Let's get out of here," she said tiredly and began the startup sequence.

I strapped into my seat, stunned by what had happened. A tree spoke to me. And asked me for help. How could I help it? I didn't even know a thing about Evo or the Ancient One. And why had it made me sick?

"Mila," I asked, "How do I get back to Evo?" Her eyes widened in alarm, so I continued, "There's something I… saw there. I want to go back. Sometime."

"You don't go back," she said, firing up the engines. "It's taken me three years to get on that spacestation, and it was the mere chance of meeting you to get me the invite."

"Oh." My heart sank. Could I never go back to help the Ancient One? It didn't seem possible. *No,* I told myself, *I would save that tree.* It might not be today or tomorrow, but I would work out how to help it.

"Where are we headed?" I asked.

Mila pulled up the sleeve of her jumpsuit. She looked at a note she'd scrawled on the inside of her arm and read, '*Prema.*'

Mila began the countdown to the docking release.

There was a knot in my stomach. I was sure that note about the planet Prema wasn't there before we'd docked on Evo station. What had Mila been doing while I was there? And why?

***

The trip to Prema would take a day with the hyper-drive, Mila told me, as we glided away from the spacestation. "From there, you can begin your pilgrimage,"

"Okay," I said into my headset. While I was already technically on my pilgrimage because I was off-world, it felt like this new planet was the actual start of my pilgrimage.

Mila made some adjustments to the tablet on the ship's dashboard. "We're on autopilot," she announced and headed to engineering again to check everything was operating smoothly. Still, she kept her headset on, so she could hear any incoming comms or alerts.

After the engine was checked, Mila announced she was going to sleep. She waved an arm at the direction of the navcontrols and said, "Don't touch anything."

She closed the door to her quarters, and all that was left was the hum of the ship's engine and the air recycler. I was thankful for the silence. It had been a long day.

I sat on the floor behind the pilot bay–or the rec room, as Mila had called it–to meditate and recenter.

The cold metal against my legs gave me goose-pimples. I shut my eyelids to connect to the sounds around me. I was used to connecting with an entire forest–with birds calling, lizards skittering by and a breeze through the treetops. I usually could smell rain and the pine scent of the forest. This ship seemed devoid of smell, other than that faint smell of mushrooms. All I could hear was the monotonous whirring of the ship. And, my own breathing, all alone. My chest felt hot. I pursed my lips, and attempted to focus, once again, on counting my breathing, but the more I slowed down, the events of the day came racing back.

It felt like it had been a dream. Today I'd launched into space and visited the Evo spacestation. I'd gone through their strange, staged search for the yellow flower, all while they were trying to find someone - or something. I remembered them taking a sample of my blood. Then, my connection with the Ancient One, which burned fire into my brain and asked for help. Weariness washed over me.

I had far more questions than answers. And I didn't even know where to begin to find out. It wasn't like there were any other biokin I was likely to find any time soon.

I didn't know enough about the world I was in to consider what I could do next. I'd barely even heard of Evo, but Mila had warned me about them. But Mila seemed like she had secrets too.

I knew that when I was at home, I snuck out at night time with Lian and didn't tell my parents. But that wasn't real lying. Not about anything important. My parents had always told me I could tell them anything and over dinner we'd talk about our day, whether we'd created something we're proud of, or embarrassed ourselves. We didn't have secrets. We didn't use subterfuge or deception to get what we wanted. The universe I'd stepped into felt far from home.

I wanted to be back home, curled up on the floor while my Mum braided my hair after I'd had a hard day. I wanted Dad to make me a hot cocoa with the foam in the shape of a rabbit, like the toy I had as a child.

I remembered the way they'd hugged me so tight when I told them I was leaving. Mum cried, and laughed nervously, and cried all over again. Dad rubbed my back telling me that he couldn't wait to hear about my adventures, but the warmth didn't spread to his eyes and his voice felt flat.

I wanted to ask Lian his perspective on everything. But my cheeks burned at the memory that I'd run from him without talking to him. I knew I wasn't ready to marry him, but perhaps that wasn't the best way to deliver the news. My life felt like it was splitting, like a fork in the road; on the left was a life with Lian, where I'd be the village healer, and on the right...? I supposed this pilgrimage would give me a hint of what other universe existed.

So far, this pilgrimage was nothing like anyone had ever told me about. My mother had met my father on her pilgrimage, and Sabine had talked about cities the size of our entire planet filled with art and music and feasts. She'd loved it so much; she didn't want to go home. In fact, when she did come home, she then fled in the middle of the night, back to the other life she'd built.

I, on the other hand, had ended up on a spaceship with someone who was doing something rather underhanded. Mila clearly had another agenda for going to visit Evo, other than merely transporting me. Not that it was any of my business. But I did worry that if she did something dangerous, I might get dragged into it too.

I wrapped my arms around my knees, tucking myself in close. I was in a cold metal ship traversing through a solar system I'd never seen, going to a planet I'd never heard of, with someone who kept more secrets than I was comfortable with. I was a sapling, flung into orbit. The forest couldn't protect my little leaves. The sun couldn't give me warmth. It was just me and the blackness of space.

I took a slow breath, to centre myself, to feel my oxygen entering, and leaving my lungs.

I began to cry softly and silently. The air recycler kept humming overhead. Slow and steady.□

Eight

Three hours later, I stood by Mila's door. I wanted to use the toilet, and I didn't want the extraction system to wake her if she was asleep. I was about to knock on her door, but I could hear the murmur of sleep talk, so I pulled my hand away. I leaned close to the door as I heard her whimper, *"It's too dark. It's too dark. Bianca!"*

My cheeks flushed. I withdrew and softly crept over to the bathroom. I washed my face instead.

This struggle with adapting to a new environment, my questions and my fear for the future was part of what it meant to be on pilgrimage. This was what it is to grow. Mum always said that growth came from bravery, and bravery came from knowing you were scared and doing the scary thing, anyway. So, I took a deep breath and focused on trying to occupy myself.

I spotted a vidscreen on the dashboard near the main nav controls. I'd seen these at the art gallery in Tevinter City, where different videos could play when you selected them. If I could learn something about the planet I was travelling to, perhaps I would feel more confident. Would it be ruled by a king or a queen? Or a democracy? Would they speak my language? I hoped so.

I figured out how to use the vid menu–it was the same as the art museum–but couldn't find anything on Prema. I figured it couldn't hurt to learn about other planets anyway because I might end up travelling to them one day. There was a planet that was entirely made of beachside resorts. And some planets had settlements that were deep underground. Some people lived on planets where the air was toxic, and they lived with giant glass bubbles with a city within. There was even a planet where everyone lived underwater in sunken ships.

I'd moved on to a documentary on a planet called Naas. A neighbouring world had invaded Naas because their planet had a rock that could be turned into energy when combined with an element from the home planet. Unfortunately, the people of Naas were not prepared for war. It left thousands of refugees trying to flee the world. With a limited navy, regular commuter ships were rigged as warships, and soon there was no way off-world. It became a slaughter, where not just the military were killed, but civilians. It was heartbreaking to watch.

"What are you watching?" Mila asked, silently padding out into the rec room, peering over my shoulder.

"Oh!" I started; before regaining my composure, I paused the video, "I wanted to watch some vids. To learn about other planets."

Mila raised her eyebrows, gesturing to the screen. "You're learning about Naas?"

It surprised me that she recognised the planet from just a still image. "You know this place?"

She shrugged, noncommittally, "Everyone knows about Naas. I'm surprised you don't."

"My people don't learn much about other worlds where we grow up."

"Right," she said, "Why not?"

"The forest we live in provides everything we need, so our schooling mostly covers, well, that."

"So, is that why Evo wanted to talk to a biokin? For information about your forest?"

"Evo wanted a biokin for something, I just don't know what."

"Why are you biokin so special?"

"We can connect with plants," I said, struggling, as always, to explain it. "We can feel them. And find them. Understand them."

"Ri-gh-t," said Mila, in a multi-syllabic way. "So that's why Evo wanted you? To find some plants."

I shrugged in assent. It's the reason Evo *told* me I was there. I wasn't sure what the real reason was. I didn't know her well enough to decide if I could trust with what happened with the Ancient One.

Her eyebrow arched. "Right. So, for someone who only knows how to look after trees, why are you so keen to head to space? There are zero trees up here."

"It's my pilgrimage. I am of age, so it's my time."

"Uh-huh. And how old is that exactly?"

"Six and ten," I said.

Now that I was looking at her, Mila was probably not more than eight and ten. She just carried herself in a way that seemed much older. Like she'd lived a lifetime already.

"So... Where did you learn about Naas?" I asked, changing the topic.

She paled.

I realised I had said something foolish. "I'm sorry," I stammered.

"No, you didn't know.... I am from Naas. This–" she nodded to the vidscreen, where a picture of shelled out shops was frozen on-screen "– was where I grew up."

I swallowed. It explained why Mila wasn't exactly the talkative type. And why she carried a knife.

She shook her head as if shaking off the memory. "But that's in the past," she patted the ship's navconsole gently, "I've got *Scout* now and I got out of there."

Mila stared at the floor, lost in thought. Then, she looked up sharply, obviously making a conscious effort to change the topic herself. "Are you hungry?"

My stomach growled as soon as she said it. I was surprised that I'd skipped a meal again. "I suppose so."

Mila moved over to the kitchen area and unfolded the cupboards. Once opened, they revealed a small kitchenette with a sink, fridge and oven. One cabinet even folded out to make an additional dining space. Next, she pulled a metal folding chair out from behind the cupboard and passed it to me while she unfolded her own.

She pulled out some cardboard boxes from the shelves. "I only have ready-meals," she added by way of explanation, "I usually travel alone."

"Whatever you have is fine," I said, peering at the box. It was a powdered product that turned into sludge when mixed with water. Even the image on the box looked unappetizing.

As I pulled out some bowls from the cupboard, I noticed a sealed bag of what looked like algae in the pantry. There was a handwritten recipe for seaweed soup taped to the front. "What about this?" I asked, pulling it out.

"Don't touch that," she snapped as if I was holding her diary. I put it back like it was burning. She held up the ready-meals and said, voice softer, "I'll heat these,"

We sat at the tiny fold-out table, and Mila served the steaming sludge.

"It doesn't look appetising, but it's got all the nutrients you need to keep fit and strong," she said, eating a spoonful.

I tentatively prodded at the sludge, which jiggled. I spooned some into my mouth cautiously. The texture was like gelatin, but the flavour was inspired by mushrooms, so it was... palatable. And it's not like there were other options around.

"Is this what everyone eats in space?" I asked, trying to hide the horror from my voice.

Mila smiled wryly, "If you're in deep space, yes. But I'm often on a planet and can just buy local produce. I mean, you couldn't live off this forever. Some people try to grow their vegetables in space,"

"Grow vegetables?" I asked, perking up. Was it possible to grow food in space?

Mila pointed to a cabinet on the rear wall, which, like everything, was a battered metal. "Maybe you can investigate how the grow tank works," Mila said, "It's something I've never had much luck with."

I walked over to the cabinet against the back wall and opened it up. There was what looked like a glass cabinet filled with soil, a sprinkler system and a sunlamp. There were some withering vegetables in there that I suspected Mila had attempted to grow once, unsuccessfully.

"This is the start of some great compost," I mused.

Mila laughed at this, which seemed to surprise us both because she smiled wryly. "I'm glad my failures will lead to something promising," she said dryly.

"I can take a look later," I said, joining her again in the kitchen. "I brought some seeds with me, so I could plant something for you."

"You brought seeds with you? Of course, you did," she smirked.

I sat down to finish the sludge.

I wondered who that note was from and why she ate ready-meals if she had seaweed there, ready to cook. Perhaps the recipe was from a lover? A parting gift as she left Naas?

"Do you have a betrothed?" I ventured, trying to keep my voice casual.

She coughed, her sludge missing her mouth. "A what?"

"A betrothed. Someone that you will marry?"

She frowned in confusion and answered by stringing the word out for a full three seconds, "Noooo. I don't usually stick around in one place long enough." Then after a moment, asked, "Do you?"

I paused. I wasn't sure. Lian obviously wanted to get married.

"I... might," I frowned. I recalled Lian's words. *I thought you'd come back for me.*

"Uh-huh," Mila said, blowing on the hot soup and taking a cautious bite. "And is he significantly older than you? Is your village like some kind of 'old cult leader marries all the young girls' kind of situation?"

I didn't know what this comment meant. "No?" I said, confused. I wasn't clear what the customs were in other worlds, but that wasn't one of ours. So, I went to my quarters and brought out my journal where I had made a sketch of Lian the previous summer, showing her.

"Oh, I see. He's nice. If that's your type."

I paused. *My type?* I'd never felt butterflies talking to Lian like everyone said you're meant to feel if you're in love. "I don't think he is," I said, realising it had never occurred to me to consider it from that perspective. I liked him as a friend. But was he my type? No.

Mila shrugged, "Then don't marry him. Assuming you can say no, right?"

"Yes, I already said no," I said, feeling hot.

"Oh, here we are, heartbreaker!" she laughed, which made me blush even more.

"He just took me by surprise, is all," I cried defensively.

"You don't need to explain yourself to me!" she said with a half-smile, "I've made my share of stupid decisions in my life,"

"You do seem like someone who jumps into the river without seeing how deep it is," I laughed.

"Gosh, you sound like my sister. She was always nagging me like that," she said, caught in a memory. *"'You're too smart to keep making stupid decisions,'* Bianca always used to say. But she never understood that life isn't always straightforward. It throws you multiple bad choices, and you need to pick the best of the worst choices."

"What's an example?" I asked.

"Like this trip," she breathed, eyes to the ground.

Then she stood abruptly like she wanted to change the topic and took her ready-meal bowl to the sink. She washed the container and laid it into a small stack in a cabinet. "We trade these in at a port, and they'll reuse them."

I stood and copied her, and we folded the dining table and chair away.

Mila looked out into the evening sky by the main windows. I was unsure of what to do with myself. I considered doing some sketching. I unfolded my journal to a blank page and looked about for a subject. Something with texture and shadow and depth. All the surfaces in the ship were smooth boxes. And then I noticed Mila.

"We've still got a few hours of flight time," Mila said, and she fixed her hair back and set herself down on the floor and started doing push-ups.

"One–" she counted, softly to herself, as she quickly lowered her body to the ground, up again. "Two–"

I could see now how she had managed to take down that guy in the tavern if she maintained her body with this kind of discipline each day.

"Three–" she breathed, lowering herself down, muscles taut beneath her jumpsuit. With shadows and texture and depth. I realised I was staring. I closed my notebook and walked over to the growtank to see if I could occupy myself there instead.

The soil was still reasonably healthy, despite everything. I found a packet of Evo plant nutrients nearby, which looked like it had never been opened. I switched on the sunlamp and tested the sprinkler. It was all working.

"Yes, I can work with this," I said to myself, nodding.

I went to my backpack and pulled out my envelopes of seeds from Perse. "Kronox beans to the rescue," I smiled.

Kronox beans were just the thing to make better quality soil so the next thing to plant would thrive. They also, helpfully, required little maintenance.

I turned on the sunlamp and the water system, and I smoothed out the dirt, ready for planting.

In a few weeks, the soil should be healthy again for Mila to plant other crops, and if all went well, the beans would sprout and become a tasty little snack. Perhaps I'd even see some shoots sprouting from the soil before we landed on Prema.

I poured the kronox seeds into my hand. "Make this soil strong again, my little heroes," I whispered to them as I tucked them into the soil. I prodded the last one in, and –

– *I saw fire, flames licking the air* –

–my hands felt warm, and there was a surge of energy through my fingers into the dirt. I steadied myself on the tank, hands in the dirt, and the tiny kronox beans were suddenly sprouting from the soil. I recoiled like I'd been burned. *What was happening?*

How would these beans grow so quickly? They usually took days to sprout–not seconds. Was it because we were in space? Or was it because that Ancient Tree did something to me?

I looked about to Mila, who had now moved on to sit-ups, counting between toothy breaths.

I closed the cabinet doors to the grow tank. I headed to my quarters and sat on the bed, clutching my head.

Surely, this wasn't something normal? I'd never heard of any biokin experiencing anything like this.

My parents never talked about this, Perse hadn't, and it wasn't even in any biokin myths.

Who could I ask about it? There were no biokin around, and Mila wasn't exactly chatty.

Perhaps it was just the stress of the new journey, I wondered. I was a long way from home. Maybe I just needed to give myself a break. Perhaps I just imagined things.

"I'm going to sleep," I called out to Mila, who responded with a short, "Yea -" mid sit-up.

I shut my door and leaned against the cold metal door. *Be strong, Addi;* I willed myself.

I lay in bed, shoes and all. I stared up at the ceiling, and my mind raced. Just two nights ago, I was sleeping in my bed in Nimbaii, and now I was in a tin can, hurtling through space, trying to understand what was happening. *Did I make those beans grow?*

I thought of the game I played with Sabine and Lian as kids. Rock. Feather. Stick. What did fire mean? *Power,* I thought, before passing out.

* * *

In my dream, I was in the forest back home. It was dark, and I'd climbed to the highest boughs of a tree. Wolves howled nearby. I jumped from branch to branch to make my way towards home, but the branches were thinning out, and I had nowhere to go. The wolves' howls were getting closer, and I was paralyzed with fear, caught at the top of the swaying treetops.

Then my vision bloomed into sunflowers, bright and open. Fields and fields of sunflowers and in my dream I connected with them, following their path as they shared the nutrients amongst themselves in glowing trails beneath the soil.

And then a knife slashed the sunflowers down—Mila's knife. And then Mila stood there, dripping with sweat, holding down a hooded figure with a knife poised above their neck.

Rap-rap-rap.

I sat bolt upright, startled by Mila's knocking on my door. "Landing in thirty," Mila called, and for a second, I thought that we hadn't even been to Evo yet, but then remembered the Ancient One.

I crawled out of bed, head pounding.

"Coffee?" Mila called from the kitchen, and I staggered out, nodding gratefully.

I grabbed the mug in my hands and sipped it gratefully.

"How long was I asleep?" I asked.

"About seven hours," Mila responded, checking the navconsole. She was dressed in a bright blue jumpsuit with a tan belt. Her curls were loose about her face. She looked like she had renewed energy, now that we'd almost arrived at Prema.

I headed to the bathroom and washed my face. I looked a mess, but I suppose most people landing on a new planet looked much the same.

I changed into a clean dress, but I noticed something odd about the growtank as I walked past. The cabinet looked like the metal was bulging outwards. My stomach twisted as I remembered what had happened when I planted the seeds. The fire in my mind.

"Did you touch this?" I asked, taking a closer look.

"I keep to engineering, you keep to the plants," Mila said, by way of an answer.

I opened up the cabinet, and fully ripened kronox plants burst from the growtank.

"I thought you said I was asleep seven hours!" I called to Mila.

"You were," she said, frowning, and then saw the beans. Her mouth dropped a little.

"Is this a thing you can do?" she asked, pointing to the plants.

"I... don't know," I whispered.

Nine

I closed my eyes and connected with the kronox beans. Ripples of glowing light ran between the stalks, linking them together. They seemed content with the sun lamp, had lots of nutrients and enough water. The only thing that was strange about them was that they had grown to full size in hours, not weeks. I was relieved when I linked with them. I didn't see a vision of fire again and was doubly relieved that I hadn't heard the plants whisper a cry of help.

I pulled a bean pod off the plant, shelled it, and ate it. It was crunchy and moist. Other than their accelerated growth, the beans seemed normal.

I remembered the thought I had before going to sleep. *Power.* That the Ancient One had given me power. It had sent fire through my veins and now I had the ability to... grow plants? I'd promised the Ancient One I'd help it, but I didn't even know how I'd get back to the spacestation, let alone save it.

"Time to strap in," Mila said. "Arrival in fifteen."

I shut the cabinet to the growtank, checked that everything in my quarters was stowed in the locker and headed to the co-pilot seat. I strapped in quickly, my mind caught up in my new powers. Was that it? Could I turn seeds into plants? I supposed I wouldn't starve.

The planet Prema looked bright red from a distance out the window, but as we flew closer, it turned out to be large tracts of earth were stripped bare, revealing bright red soil. The northern-most quarter of the entire planet had giant triangular machines sticking out of the surface, reaching into the stratosphere, rocking back and forth like clockwork.

"Why is it red?" I asked.

"Iron ore," Mila explained into her headset, "It makes the dirt red."

"But the *whole planet* is red. Aren't there any trees?" I asked, horrified.

"Not many. They've open-cut mined most of the surface," Mila said. She pointed out the set of machines on the northern tip of the planet. "They had to build those counterweights there. They dug up so much ore that if they didn't, the orbit around its sun would be out of whack, and it would become a frozen planet."

"*Oh.*" I suspected this wasn't one of the planets I'd heard about, which was full of holiday-makers and artists. I sighed. Pilgrimage is about exploring the universe, and not all of it would be glamorous.

"So, how do they breathe if there aren't forests?"

"I think they electrified the ocean or something," she said, "To get the oxygen out."

"What ocean?"

She pointed vaguely to one side of the planet, "Oh, well, I suppose it's not there anymore."

Mila radioed in someone at the spaceport at Claven, the largest city, who approved her path in.

"Descent in 3, 2, 1...." Mila said into her headset. She programmed in a course, and the engines roared, but in a different way to takeoff.

The descent was terrifying. The only thing in my field of vision was the planet's surface rapidly growing in our field of view. And the only person stopping us from going splat into the surface was Mila, at the steering wheel, hands rattling with the vibrating ship.

Proximity alarms were going off every minute as we drew closer to the surface. "Yeah, yeah, I know there's an object right in front of me. It's called a *planet*," Mila muttered to the alarms as we hurtled downward, the ship violently shaking as we entered the atmosphere. The roaring of the engines grew even louder, and I was worried again that I'd be sick, but nothing was left in my stomach.

We saw the spaceport below us and raced towards it at a speed that made me dizzy. What was once a distant city became buildings, and landing tarmac was just ahead. My nails dug into the seat.

As the proximity sensors turned into a loud whine, Mila pulled some levers on the dashboard up hard, throwing me forward in my seat. The engines fired up in a deafening roar, and then we were gliding down to the planet towards a landing bay.

We settled down onto the cement of the runway with a less-than-dainty thump. We'd made it.

***

I climbed down the main exit of the *Scout* and took a deep breath of the city of Claven's air. It was hot here. It was a dry heat, and waves of it radiated off the tarmac. The planet Prema smelled so different from home. Here, I could smell tobacco, oil and liquor. It was not the pine-scented air of Nimbaii.

The spaceport looked much more industrial than in Tevinter. There were no beautifully tiled aisles, just cold hard cement and large trolleys with what looked like rocks being shipped in and out. I gasped as a robot man was pushing a trolley. I pointed it out to Mila, but she just rolled her eyes. A logo with the word Dervin was plastered over nearly every object around.

"Is that the name of this city?" I asked.

"No, it's the company that owns the planet."

A company? Owning a whole planet? There was a lot I had to learn about the universe.

My heart sank. It felt so strange that there were almost no forests here. I'd spent my entire life surrounded by trees, and this place felt so exposed and empty, even surrounded by buildings. But every culture was different, and as I was starting my pilgrimage here, I was sure there was something here I'd learn to love.

We headed into the spaceport, and Mila logged our arrival with docking control, which had its own Dervin logo. There was a balding man at a small perspex window, which was covered in notifications of what you could, or couldn't, bring into Prema. Llamas were, apparently, forbidden, but goats, acceptable. One notice—again with Dervin logo—read 'PORT FEE: 500 CREDITS', and below that, in handwriting, someone had written, 'If you don't pay the fee, you don't leave the planet.'.

While Mila spoke to the man—her conversation getting more and more heated—I looked around me as men in dark overalls bustled across the port delivering cargo. Hawkers were selling fried noodles, and rows of bright, musical machines captivated men in yellow uniforms, who were feeding them tokens in a trance. Men walked out of dimly lit rooms adjusting their belts, beneath a sign reading 'Comfort House'. Was that a bathroom?

After a red-faced discussion, Mila marched over to me. She waved her arm around the spaceport grandly. "Welcome to Prema. I'm sure you can find your way from here. Ping me the credits you owe me for this transport, and we're square."

I hesitated. When I'd made the agreement with Mila about paying her the 300 credits for the transport, I thought I would have the money from Evo to pay her. But they said they would take three months to pay. And at this exact moment, I only had 200 credits. In fact, less than that—thanks to the cider I'd had with Lian.

At my hesitation, Mila folded her arms, eyes narrowing. "We agreed that you would pay me 300 credits when we landed. You're here. *Landed.*"

"I don't have all the credits," I said, trying to keep my voice calm to avoid this becoming an argument involving knives.

Her mouth gaped open a little. "Excuse me? You agreed to 300 credits. I wouldn't have landed if you didn't have the money."

"I thought I would get some credits from Evo," I explained.

She looked as if her worst nightmare was coming true. "How much *do* you have?"

"I have 190," I said, wincing.

She closed her eyes and started moaning under her breath, "No, no, no, no." Her eyes bored into the docking fee sign of 500 Credits. Mila didn't have enough credits to leave the planet. She'd been riding on me paying her immediately.

Then her eyes snapped open with determination. "Okay. Change of plan. You are going to get me my 300 credits. *Today.*"

She herded me over to a nearby noticeboard. "This is the greyboard," she explained, "You can find work here." It was a digital board with a black screen and green font, with text notices rotating every few minutes. She stood back, scanning the posts. There were job vacancies. Transport. Mining. Construction. Chef. Exotic dancers. I wondered how far away your planet needed to be for you to be considered 'exotic'.

"Maybe," Mila muttered under her breath as she scanned the notices, "You can make a money tree grow and then we'll be fine." I ignored that barb.

There were notices for missing persons and bounties. "Good to see we don't have a bounty on us," Mila muttered, and I wondered why she'd even think that.

One notice read "Meeting, 1pm, Walsh Public House: Union Against Robotics," while another read, "Join the ASR–Alliance for Sentient Robots. Meet Tuesdays at Sano Cafe." It was like I'd opened up a book and started right in the middle. Why was there so much conflict about robots?

She prodded a finger at a news item about a team of Evo scientists who were doing some research underground and had gone missing from Prema a few days ago. "I wonder if..." she said to herself, then, looking around, spotted a local food vendor. "Don't go anywhere."

I watched her approach the middle-aged man and ask something about the greyboard. They spoke for a minute, and, after some awkward gestures between them, Mila rolled her eyes and bought a cup of noodles. On her way back to me, she dumped the noodles in the compost bin.

"There are usually Evo scientists on Prema all the time, but at the moment, these missing scientists are the only ones on the planet."

"Oh-kay?"

"Because there is no one else from Evo here right now, they're contracting out the rescue. There's a reward of 500 credits."

"I don't think that's something I can help with," I said. It's not like we were a rescue team. We weren't even a team.

Mila was silent, lost in thought.

I pointed to one notice I thought I could help with: *AGRISCIENTIST WANTED. Consultant required to test soil quality.*

Mila raised an eyebrow. "You're not an agriscientist."

"No, but I can find out what's wrong with the soil from the plants that are there. I can do this job." I stabbed a finger at one line. It also paid 400 credits.

I suspected that if Mila hadn't seen the kronox beans spring up overnight, I don't imagine she'd have believed me. I didn't dissuade her assumption that I could grow food overnight on purpose. I figured that it didn't hurt to have her thinking that I had some kind of power. She had the ship, credits and knew how to use a knife. I was using the only leverage I had: my new secret powers. Not that I knew what they did, yet.

"Okay, let's go." She announced. To my surprise, she said, "I'm coming with you. I'm not leaving your side until you pay my credits." She gestured at my long cotton dress and woven bag, "Besides, no one is going to take you seriously as an agriscientist in that outfit."

I looked down, "What's wrong with my outfit?"

Mila acted as if she hadn't heard me. Instead, she looked at her navcomm and checked the time. "They are located a fair way out of town. We'd better leave now if we are going to get there while it's still daylight."

We left the grimy spaceport and followed the signs to a nearby high-speed rail station. Mila stabbed a finger at the map, to a place at the end of the line. "This is where we're headed."

On the train platform, Mila called the man who posted the job ad to confirm that the job was still available and that the fee was still 400 credits. She told them we'd be there this afternoon.

Around us, men in fluorescent coloured clothing jammed onto the platform. Mila bought two return tickets for us, and we climbed aboard the next train.

"In case you're keeping a tally," she said dryly, "You now owe me 306 credits."

The train was smooth and fast, even if it was an older model. The trains were air-conditioned, and compared to the dry heat outside, it was freezing on the train. The seats were crowded, and we needed to stand for most of the trip. The view outside was what biokin would have considered a wasteland. The few forests were mostly stripped to the ground. Gaping holes for open-cut mining dominated the landscape. It looked like whole forests were burning.

My skin started to feel clammy. If I was planning to talk to plants to find out what was happening on this farm, I needed some plants with which to speak. There might not be any here. I crossed my fingers, hoping I'd be able to do this job.

Station by station, workers disembarked at platforms that were set up by their respective mining operations. From there, other transport systems waited to take them further afield for their work.

As we travelled toward across the planet, the landscape changed, and it looked like we were in a rare agricultural area. While it was certainly not enough to feel the planet, it was reassuring that some plants were on the surface.

By the final station, we were almost the only people disembarking at an unmanned train platform. Mila consulted her navcomm and squinted against the sun to an old farmhouse behind a field of what looked like corn. "That's the address."

***

We walked along a road approaching the farmhouse, and the corn was looking like it would mature in a few days. The soil was bright red, but it didn't seem to make a difference to the corn. I wondered what was wrong with it for us to come out here.

The cornfield was only a small farm, but it would be a good yield. On the edge of the field, was a small hill with another homestead on the other side. Despite being so far from the city, there were a few people who lived out here.

We approached the farmhouse, and Mila rang an old bell by the front door.

We heard someone run down some stairs from inside, calling out, "Coming!". A girl around our age flung open the door, and as her eyes fell on us, her smile turned to a thin line.

"*Oh,*" she said.

"We're here to test the soil," Mila announced in her professional voice. "Is Mr. Imai here?"

She sighed, "Yeah, come on in." She led us into a sitting room and yelled up the stairs, "*Daaad!*"

We took a seat, and she folded her arms. "You're the soil experts? We're completely screwed."

Mila looked unruffled, "My colleague here has been working with plants for over a decade. In fact, we've just come from consulting with Evo."

The girl rolled her eyes, "Better not let Dad hear you say that. Evo is not too popular around here. They're our biggest competitor and all."

She pointed to a screen embedded in the wall with a list of rankings. "Everyone is pretty competitive around here."

"Is that a list of farms on the planet?" Mila asked, frowning.

"Yes. You get paid if you're above this line," the girl said, indicating on the chart. "You get points for speed, the yield, all kinds of things. If you don't get enough points, you don't get paid."

"You - you don't get paid for your own crops?" I asked, aghast.

"It's just how it works around here. We've always been above the line. Until this year, at least," the girl said bitterly.

Mila nodded at the coffee table with a stack of engineering textbooks and drawings of mechanical limbs on paper. "Are you an engineer?"

"Not if we don't get this crop fixed."

"Why is that?" I asked.

"I'm *meant* to go to university this season. But instead, I need to pay off our debt to the company store. So, I'm being sent to the mines. Or more likely, a Comfort House."

"A what?" I asked.

"It's where-"

"No one's going to a Comfort House," said a voice from the top of the landing. Mr. Imai, I presumed, hobbled down the stairs. He had greying hair and a robotic leg which I tried hard not to stare at.

Mila stood, walked over to meet him and shook his hand. "Mr. Imai. I'm Mila Riley, and this is the soil consultant, Addison Nora. We spoke on the comm."

He nodded, gesturing we sit back down.

"Thanks for coming out here. I know it's rather unconventional that I advertise on the greyboard for a soil specialist–but I'm in a bit of a bind. I need to hire someone–discreetly–to fix this crop. If the company finds out I've hired someone, they might think I can't do my job, I get demerits, and..." he gestured vaguely to the board on the wall.

Mila nodded, "We can be discreet. The payment is 400 credits?"

Mr. Imai nodded while the girl shifted uncomfortably as if that price had been an argument she'd lost.

"Now, let's get to business. We need to get this crop sorted. I've been running this farm for fifteen years. I grow corn for Derwin, and I get paid when I deliver the crop. But this crop, as you can see, hasn't matured. The stalks are there, but there's *no corn*. It hasn't begun tasseling *at all*." Mr. Imai started nervously rolling his thumbs together. "The first few weeks, I thought it was just taking its time, so I borrowed some money from the company store for food and bills. But it's been like this for nearly ten weeks. It should usually take ten *days*. I need a crop to deliver soon, or I will be sent to the mines to repay the debts."

"You won't be sent to hard labour, Dad," the girl said, gesturing to his leg. "*I* will."

He looked at her sharply to silence her.

"So, as you can see, getting this crop to yield is important for us. We can't work out why this year the corn isn't growing. It's the same seed we've always used. We've done every test we can think of, which is why we wanted to bring in an expert."

My heart dropped. This family was in a bind. What if I couldn't help these people? What if I talked to their plants and learned nothing? What if they never could repay the debt, and they'd be sent off to the mines or whatever a Comfort House was. I let a slow breath out. *You can do this.*

"Let's take a look at your crop," I said, standing.

Mr. Imai led us out to the cornfield while the girl stayed inside, arms folded, peering out through the kitchen window.

The day was still hot even though it was nearing dusk, and the red soil stained my boots as we walked out into the cornfield.

I squatted down and felt the soil. It was a little more delicate than the soil I had back home, but it was still the same thing.

I remembered all the scientists on the spacestation with their equipment. Mr. Imai might think I'm a scam artist if I just sat there with my eyes closed–especially if they'd never heard of biokin. So, I pulled off my backpack to pretend to get some instruments from my bag and sent a meaningful look to Mila.

She turned to the farmer, "You don't have any coffee, do you?"

"Sure. Give me a minute," Mr. Imai nodded, then headed over to his farmhouse.

"You've probably got five minutes to do whatever it is you do before he is back."

I nodded, and I placed my fingers on the nearest corn stalk.

I breathed in the hot air and the earthy scent of soil. The buzz of crickets was drowned by the grinding of machinery from the mining work on the other side of the train tracks. I breathed in. And out. And I was in. The corn stalks lit up like they were phosphorescent. In my vision, rows and rows of corn lit up all across the farm.

I could sense their discomfort, the feeling of disgust. *Of poison.*

I needed to find the source of the poison, so I extended my awareness to the next row of corn and the next.

I pushed myself to keep following the network, along each row. Then, suddenly, the system I was connected to wasn't just the cornfield, but to the trees on the field's far edge and to the moss and fungi below the ground.

I kept following the connection, further and further than I'd ever extended before. Then, my reach was over the hill and deep underground.

Reaching this vast distance was something else new that I could do since my visit to Evo.

And then I heard it.

Tap-Tap-Tap-pause-*Tap*-pause-*Tap*-pause-*Tap*-pause-*tap-tap-tap.*
What was that?

Tap-Tap-Tap-pause-*Tap*-pause-*Tap*-pause-*Tap*-pause-*tap-tap-tap.*

It was far away, a tiny sound. What could that be? I tried to follow the signal, but it was deep underground.

"Addison?"

I was wrenched out of the network.

"What?" I frowned.

"You were tapping," Mila said. "With your fingers, you were tapping a code."

"It's... something I heard. Underground. I think one of the plants there can hear it and is relaying it through the network."

"... Do you know what that code means, Addison?"

And I shook my head, irritated, wanting to sink back into the network. She interrupted my focus.

"It's a code. Someone is calling for help."□

Ten

I paled. Was that code a cry for help from deep underground?

"It's something I remember from Naas," she explained softly. And then her eyes grew wide, "Do you think it could be the science team that went missing?"

I shrugged. "I could only hear the code. I don't know anything else."

Mila spotted Mr. Imai heading over to us, carrying two mugs of coffee. I stood up and dusted off my dress and tried to look as if I was inspecting the soil as a scientist would.

"Any luck?"

I paused processing what I'd experienced in my meditation. I remember the corn in the field was aching with poison. And some saplings were, too, on the border of the property. But I remember that the old trees beyond them were unaffected. I got to my feet and nodded to the treeline on the small hill. "We need to go there."

We headed over to the trees on the boundary of the farm. "These are my neighbour's trees," he explained, wary that we'd crossed the property border. There was nothing out of place on the hill–just a neat row of grass and saplings.

I fell to my knees and began digging in the dirt. I clawed away handfuls of grass and dirt as I began to dig.

"Oh, Addison!" Mila exclaimed in horror, and she put her hand on my shoulder to restrain me, but I kept pulling out fistfuls of dirt. "Addison!" And then I hit it. What I'd been searching for. A hose. I dragged it from the soil. I kept pulling it, and dirt dislodged from all along the hillside on either side of us. The hose sprinkled dirt over us as it was hauled from its hiding place in the hillside. The hose followed the whole border of the property. It had holes drilled into it all the way along to let out the poison at intervals.

Mr. Imai gasped.

"This hose has been seeping poison into your field," I explained.

"My neighbour! He's been poisoning my field?! We tested for poison!"

"If it's something organic like salt, it might not have come up on the test, but it will still cripple your plants."

"But why? We—we work for the same company!" His face drained as he started inspecting the hose. "Unless... My daughter has been developing some machines to help me manage the crops when she's at university. He—hates robots. He might think I'll outrank him. But really, if I can't pay back this debt, my business is gone. I'll never come back from it." He turned to me, eyes watering. "Thank you. There is a company policy for this, and I can get my debts wiped. You've saved my daughter from a terrible fate."

Mila eyes settled on me, a soft smile on her lips.

"Not bad, biokin," Mila said, beaming. My heart gave a jump.

She turned to Mr. Imai. "We've got a few other projects this afternoon. If this job is to your satisfaction, please ping the 400 credits."

We walked to the house, and he paid us. Mila looked radiant.

And now, Mila and I were square. She'd go her way, and I'd go mine. And I now had a hundred credits of my own, too.

I wasn't sure how much a hotel would be back in the city, but hopefully, I'd could get a room for the night. Then, tomorrow, I could find another job or see if there were any other planets in this system that I might want to visit. It was one step at a time.

We walked alongside the cornfields on the way to the train station.

Mila grabbed my arm, pulling me to face her.

"Listen," she hissed, "I need to find those scientists," I remembered the ones listed on the greyboard. "That code you heard in the field requesting help might be them. Do you–think you could track them?"

What was Mila up to? I was getting tired of Mila's secrets. The errand she needed to run on Evo. Why she even needed to come to Prema at all. "Why do you want to find this science team so much?"

Her eyes narrowed. "Can't I be motivated by the joy of saving lives?" Then, after I let that silence sit for a full half-minute, she said, "I'll cut you in 50/50 on the reward."

Ah. I thought. Was it as simple as the fact that Mila still needed credits to pay her docking fee? Mila had a habit of telling things that seemed like half-truths, so it was hard to pull apart the threads and find complete lies. In the end, I wasn't sure we even could find them, but my new powers might help guide us.

I folded my arms, "Okay. But no guarantees. I've never done anything like this before."

She grinned like the sun emerging from behind a cloud. "Thank you, Addison," she said.

I pointed to a metal object set in the ground a few metres from us.

"You want to go underground? There's a wastewater system entrance."

And Mila closed her eyes, just for a moment, bracing herself, before nodding.

My mother had been an architect, so while I hadn't seen many wastewater systems in person, I had a pretty good idea what they were like. Thanks to her, I'd seen many vids on the subject as a child.

It took both of us to remove the metal grate from the wastewater system, and then we climbed down into the tunnel. It was like a lot of wastewater systems I'd seen in vids–it was a tunnel large enough to fit a few horses, with wastewater running down the centre.

This looked like a main access tunnel, so it had a small metal walkway suspended above the water. There was lighting every few metres. I thanked the Ancients that the walkway meant we didn't need to touch the wastewater yet.

"Which way do we go?" Mila asked, surveying the space.

I tried to orient myself from where we were at the farm, but I wasn't sure where we were facing since we headed underground. The only way I would have an idea of which direction to head was if I could connect with plants again. There was a crack in the cement of the wall with a piece of moss growing on it. Thank the Ancients–I could use it to connect to the network.

"Hey, little fellow," I cooed to the moss. "Can you tell me where to go?"

Mila's silence told me that she wasn't sure how long she'd put up with too much weirdness from me–even if I was helping her find credits. I paused, exhaling, trying to stop my thoughts racing and connect with a space of calm. The cement was cool, and nearby water dripped into the larger body of water moving at a glacial pace. I connected with the moss. The air was moist and dank. Beyond the cement, worms and bugs were going about their day. I extended my awareness further. There was the *tap-tap-tap* again. It was getting easier to connect with plants. I tried to shrug off the thought that this was a new benefit of connecting with the Ancient One on the Evo spaceship.

"It's this direction." I pointed, and Mila programmed the direction into her navcomm as a reference.

We headed along the path for a few minutes until we reached a fork in the tunnels. Mila consulted her navcomm and faced the north-most tunnel. "I think this is the best route."

This tunnel was smaller, and now we couldn't avoid walking in some of the wastewater around our boots. I winced as I stepped into the tunnel, but my shoes didn't immediately fill with water. I could tell we were moving from the central maintenance tunnels to just regular sewerage pipes. This tunnel was narrower, and the cement was coarse.

"Remember," Mila hummed to herself, "A lot of this is just rainwater."

I privately disagreed, as Mila looked much less comfortable underground than she had above ground. I wondered if she didn't like small spaces.

We walked for what must have been thirty minutes with little discussion in this direction when we felt a slight tremor from the pipes surrounding us.

"What was that?" I asked.

"It's a tremor. Remember that this is a mining planet. They do excavations and controlled explosions here every day."

I didn't point out that the people we were searching for were probably lost due to a 'controlled explosion', but I didn't think it would help the situation.

Another tremor rocked the tunnel more forcefully. The lighting pulsed off and then on again. Mila jumped when the lights flickered. "How much further? I don't want to be here in the dark."

We started scrambling down the tunnel faster, but soon there was another tremor, and the lights switched off and didn't turn back on.

Mila froze. Her breath had become a cycle of slow, forced inhale, a pause, then a lengthy exhale. She was gripping my arm so tight it hurt.

"Are you okay?" I asked.

She activated her navcomm, and there was a dull glow, which lit her face. But it certainly did not reach any further.

"I–I don't like confined spaces," she stammered. Then I remembered what I'd overheard on the ship when she'd been asleep. She'd been afraid of the dark. But when she spoke, her voice was taut with panic. "I can't believe how stupid we were to come here without getting gear first. I was just in such a rush to find–" and she stammered "–the scientists. I didn't even think about what would happen if we got trapped down here."

"We're not trapped," I said. "We'll be okay,"

This was much easier than going caving, I thought, because we're in a big wide tunnel with only forward or backwards. Back home, we'd been caving a lot (especially since Lian wanted to find that moonshine). Cave tunnels split and converged like a bag of snakes. You thought you were on the one path, but you'd turn off to go somewhere wholly different only to end up in a cave so small you couldn't move or you would find yourself returning to where you started. The only way we knew how to find our way around them was to -

"Wait," I called, rummaging around in my backpack. My fingers caught the rubbery fungus and pulled the object out of my medicine bag.

"What are you doing?" hissed Mila.

"Just wait," I said, holding up the mushroom. I gently blew on the surface of the mushroom, and its spores opened up. And it transformed into a torch, lighting up the tunnel as far as we could see. Mila's skin lit up bright blue as I held it above us.

"What is that?" Mila gasped.

"It's a bioluminescent mushroom. We have these all over my planet. So, I keep one handy for, well, situations like these."

"It's... amazing."

We stared at the mushroom, captivated.

"Now, we can see."

Her tight grip on my arm relaxed as she forced herself to take deep breaths to calm down.

"Of course you've got a plant instead of a real torch," she muttered and was obviously feeling more sure of herself again.

"Let's keep going," I said, leading the way in the blue light as Mila's navcomm blinked out.

We walked like this for perhaps another forty minutes. My shoes had started to get soggy with the wastewater trickling by, and I'd begun to feel cold. The dank air no longer bothered me. My stomach rumbled, and I remembered the last meal I had of the terrible soup on Mila's ship. It already felt a lifetime ago.

Mila paused, grabbing my arm for me to stop walking. "Do you hear that?"

"Hear what?"

I held my breath. I heard a quiet, metallic *tap-tap-tap*.

"*It's the code calling for help!*" She breathed. "I can hear them!"

Her eyes sparkling; she squeezed past me and started racing down the tunnel. The sound of the banging grew louder as we ran. "Come on!" she cried as her pace nearly turned into a sprint.

I chased after her, holding the mushroom aloft so we could see.

Tap-tap-tap.

"Hurry!" she cried, footsteps splashing in the water as she ran. She was running right on the cusp of my blue light. Mila was nearly out of my vision and then paused in her tracks.

The pipe had ended in a sheer drop, overlooking a large room. I ran into Mila, almost shoving her right off the edge.

It was another junction, where several large pipes flowed into this room, water trickling in. There was an exit pipe at the other side of the room below us, but there had been a rockfall on the far side. The water was seeping through the rockfall, trying to escape.

We could hear the metallic code banging even louder now, just metres away.

"Hello?!" Mila called, voice with a kind of hope I'd never heard.

We heard a muffled cry of "Is someone there?" from somewhere around us. *Tap-tap-tap.*

"Yes!" Mila called. "We're coming!"

"Hello?" the voice shouted. "Hello? Can you hear us?"

"We hear you!" Mila cried even louder. "We're coming for you!"

There was a hoot of joy from–somewhere.

But we still couldn't see them.

"Where are they?" Mila asked anxiously, eyes darting about the room below us.

We climbed down into the room but couldn't find where the scientists were. They must have been somewhere off from one of the surrounding tunnels.

"Can you do your plant thing to find them again?"

I handed the glowing mushroom to Mila and looked about the room for some plants I could connect with. I found some exposed dirt near the rockfall, and I dug around until I found a root from a tree overhead.

I shut my eyes and listened to the room we stood in. Water was trickling in from the pipes in the walls, my shoes were sodden with water, I started to shiver. But we were so close to finding them. *Focus,*

I told myself. I exhaled and felt the rough root in my hands, the cool, soft soil it was bulging out of, the coarse rocks about it.

I connected with the root, and the network of plants lit up in my vision. They formed a constellation, reaching far up overhead, far behind us, and all around us. But ahead of us, behind the rockfall, layers of moss were scattered along uneven cave surfaces and then as I followed the link, there were no plants at all. "I think there's a natural cave behind this rockfall," I said.

Mila pursed her lips. "They must have got trapped there when this rockfall happened."

"How are we going to get to them?" I asked, looking at the pile of boulders blocking off the path, not seeing how we could move them. Mila was sizing them up to see if she could lift them, but she wasn't that strong.

And then the earth started shaking, and rocks began falling from the ceiling.

Eleven

An enormous boulder fell in front of me, and I yelped, leaping back and covering my head. Clumps of dirt and rocks fell over the room, and Mila leapt over to me. She pulled me close to protect me from the debris.

Rocks and chunks of cement fell about us, splashing into the water to the left and right of us. Buckets of dirt showered us, and we crouched together, her arms tight around my back. The shaking finally stopped, and the tremor had dislodged something in the sewerage system above us. The sound of water was rushing in. A pipe had burst, blocking the exit we had come in through. The tunnel with the rockfall was now completely blocked, and water could no longer escape. Now, water was creeping up over our ankles and rising.

"Addi, help me move these rocks!" Mila began throwing the smaller rocks off the pipe that had the cave behind it. We made some headway clearing the rubble. Mila indicated a boulder we should move together, and she readied herself to lift on one side, and I grabbed the other. We pushed the rock a foot before it no longer budged. "Come on again!" Mila said, counting down, and we moved the rock another foot. This was a baby rock compared to the other boulders blocking the way to the cave. Mila started looking concerned.

"How are we going to move the bigger rocks if we can't even move these smaller ones?" she asked.

I looked around. There was nothing we could use as leverage, like a branch or a loose pipe. "I don't know," I confessed.

"We have to get through!"

"I know! But what we can do? Can we call for help on your nav-comm?"

Mila looked at the silent device. "No reception here. I bet that's why the mining team didn't call themselves."

We were really in trouble now. The water kept flowing and was lapping our calves. If this didn't stop, we'd drown down here.

"Can't you just magic up a tree branch or something?" Mila cried. "You made all that freaking corn or whatever in the growtank–can't you–make a tree that can lift all this stuff out of the way."

I snapped, "Mila! *I don't do magic*!"

"Then what did you do in my growtank, huh?!" her eyes glowered.

I realised that I'd made a mistake by implying that I had control over these new powers.

"Mila," I said, "I can't do that-"

"Oh, come *on*! Don't mess me around! Just do it! Can't you see we're going to be trapped here if we don't move?"

"Mila..." I took in a deep breath. "I didn't make the kronox beans grow. Well, I did, but I didn't. I... don't know how it happened."

"What do you mean?"

"I can't make plants *grow*."

She folded her arms, eyes ablaze. "*Bull*. I saw what happened with those beans!"

"*I didn't do it on purpose*!" I cried. "Something happened to me on the Evo spacestation. I... connected with this tree, and now I can do things I couldn't do before."

Mila's eyes narrowed. "You were experimented on by Evo, and now you've got magic powers, and *you didn't think to mention it?*"

"It wasn't like that!" I said, "They didn't know it happened. There was a tree there, and it spoke to me, and I vomited, and now it looks like I have powers where plants sometimes grow."

"I can't believe you would keep this a secret! Do you know how dangerous Evo is? Do you have any idea what they would do to you if they found out you left their lab with magic powers?"

"*Me*? Keeping secrets?!" I spat, "*You* are the one who has been do-ing everything in secret! It's obvious we're not rescuing these scientists because of the credits! You're looking for something! And you stole something at Evo! I don't know if it was an object or information–but you wouldn't even look at me until you realised I was your way in. *You used me.* If anyone here is full of secrets–it's you. And now–*now*–we're going to die down here because you are keeping secrets!"

Mila's cheeks paled, and she was silent for a full minute.

"I didn't know if I could trust you," she said quietly, which, I noticed, wasn't an apology. And then she took a deep breath. "The real reason I'm here is that my sister is missing. She's an Evo scientist, and she's been missing for three years. I'm... trying to find her." She started wringing her hands. "I've tried to find her through the official channels, but everyone claims she's never been on Evo staff. Which is not true. She got off Naas but I haven't heard from her since she got the job with Evo. I've been following rumours of her for years. Every few months she's sent to a new planet for work. So, yes, I used you to get into Evo because I thought I could see where she was now, rather than following a cold trail. I borrowed the access pass of that scientist I met there to look at their internal staff records. The records said she arrived here on Prema two weeks ago. And... as these scientists here are the only Evo people on the planet, I thought she might be here. That's why I'm here. To find my sister."

My cheeks burned. Yes, Mila had kept the truth from me. But it was also her business. And it seemed like she had a good reason for keeping her secret, especially if Evo were as dangerous as she says.

"Cripes," I breathed. "I'm so sorry your sister has gone missing."

Mila's voice croaked as her eyes welled with tears. "This is the closest I've ever come to finding her in three years."

The water lapped at our knees now.

"Let's save your sister," I whispered. She nodded, wiping a tear from her eye, then her usually steely expression returned.

I waded over to the edge of the rockfall to find the roots I'd felt earlier. Mila had asked me to use my power to summon a tree to move the rocks. Was this new power something I could control? I had to try.

I grabbed the roots in my hands, and I closed my eyes. The root was course in my palm. I could smell concrete and dirty water. I began to shiver. The water was chilly and the noise of more water flooding in was deafening. Water was rushing in, and in my mind, it was rushing up to our legs–gushing up to drown us–

"I can't do it!" I cried.

"Yes, you can!" Mila hissed, walking over to me and putting her hand on my shoulder, grip fierce.

"I can't focus!" There was too much noise, too much water, too much going on in my head.

"Focus on me," she grabbed my other hand, standing close.

I exhaled. Mila's soft hand was in the palm of mine, her cold skin against mine. Her wild, curly hair tickled my neck. And her hot breath was against my skin. The other sounds in the cave disappeared. The root I was touching started glowing in my vision. I was connected to the network.

All around the room, the tree roots surrounded us. And, beyond that, the trees reached all the way up to the surface, all around for miles.

"Please, Ancient Ones, lend me your strength," I whispered. "Move these rocks."

The network all around that all the trees were connected to surrounded us, and a jolt of electricity pulsed through my fingers from distant trees lending me their strength. I saw a vision of a tall, ancient tree, taller than the surrounding forest.

"Yes, *help us*!" I whispered.

There was a spark of heat and a tingling in my fingers. And then the roots surrounding us in the cave began to grow. They bulged and twisted, becoming the thickness of watermelons, like hundred-year-old roots. And the roots started to shift the rocks. The wastewater found a gap to creep through and began pouring out from the cave, the cold water crept away from my legs. The roots kept growing and hauled the boulders aside, Mila's heart raced against me, gripping my fingers tight. Her breath on my neck. Her skin, covered in goose-pimples, shivered against mine.

"You did it," she whispered.

And I opened my eyes. The boulders had been hauled clear of the pipe, and the water was flowing through, the exit clear. The wastewater was lowering from our calves.

"Thank you, Ancient Ones," I whispered to the trees which had loaned their strength.

"Is that a new thing you can do now?" she asked.

"I... asked the trees to help. They didn't need to, but they did."

"Thank you," she said, and I wasn't sure if she was talking to me or the trees.

She unwrapped her arms from around me and clambered over the fallen boulders. She peered into the pipe leading to the cave.

"Hello?" she called.

"Hello!" voices echoed back, jubilant. "We're in here!"

Mila looked at me, a smile faint on her lips. "I guess we're going in."

I unwrapped one of the long tree roots from the boulder and handed it to her like a rope. "We might need this," I said.

She smiled a half-grin. "Look at us! We might get out of this alive in the end."

"We might just."

She picked up the glowing mushroom and held it aloft, and she started walking down the pipe into the darkness beyond.

Clambering over boulders, she came to the end of the pipe. Or, at least, what was now the end, because it had collapsed into the cave. There was a natural cave below us, and the pipe had split and fallen into it.

The group of scientists had set up a camp below us, with blankets and lighting illuminating the cave above in yellows and blues. They waved toward us as they saw our light. There were two women and two men.

The drop down wasn't that far down–maybe six feet–but with the rock collapse, they still would have been trapped even if they had been able to climb up.

"Hello!" Mila called down to them.

"We are so glad to see you!" one man called back, who was thin as a reed.

"How did you find us?" a woman with short-cropped blonde hair called.

"We heard your code requesting help!" Mila said.

"Yes! *I told you it would work*!" the other man held a pipe in the air in a victory stance and banged an off-key celebratory tune on the metal pipes above him.

Mila threw the long root down the edge of the pipe like a rope and started climbing down to them. "Are you the Evo science team?"

"We are! We lost comms when the tunnel collapsed. I can't believe you heard us! Are you the rescue team?"

"Kind of. We were just nearby when we heard your signal."

"Evo didn't send you?" the other woman asked, voice cracking. She had black hair and thick glasses.

"Sort of," she said weakly.

"Is anyone hurt?" I called, getting ready to pull my medicine bag out of my backpack.

"No," the man with the pipe sighed, "We're fine. Just exhausted."

Mila started climbing down the long root to meet them. I looked about the group, but none had the hair and eyes of Mila. Her sister wasn't there. Mila's voice caught in her throat. "Is this the entire team?"

"Yes," the blonde woman confirmed. "This is our whole team."

Mila was silent for a moment, lost in her private grief.

I called down, "Can you follow us back up?"

"Yes. Let's go," the reedy man agreed. Their desire to escape the cave was stronger than their exhaustion.

The team abandoned most of their equipment–Evo could come back for it later–but brought their headlamps with them to see.

"Is... that a bioluminescent mushroom?" the woman with the glasses asked, frowning.

"It is," Mila confirmed, making a boost with her hands for the woman to climb up the makeshift rope.

I hauled them, one by one, into the pipe and pointed out the path through to the main junction room we'd come from. The scientists began to clamber through.

Mila finally climbed up the root herself, and I pulled her up the last foot.

"I'm sorry about your sister," I whispered, hauling her onto the landing.

She pursed her lips.

"I'm not giving up yet," she whispered back. "She might not be here, but I'm sure she's alive."

As they made their way to the junction room, the scientists looked around them at the engorged root system. "What the heck? Did the tremors do this?" one asked.

"I guess so," Mila said quickly.

The access ladder was nearby and hadn't been damaged in the rock-fall, and the water had stopped flooding the room, so we clambered back up into the tunnels we'd used to get here. In these smaller pipes, the men had to stoop uncomfortably, lagging behind.

I led the way carrying the mushroom at the head of the group, and Mila was behind me, talking to the women.

"I just can't believe our luck," the woman with the glasses breathed, "Were you hunting for mushrooms when you heard us? I can't believe you came down here without any equipment!"

Mila smiled wanly, "It's an exercise we won't be repeating, believe me!".

"But seriously, how can we repay you?"

"Well," Mila shifted instantly into businesswoman mode, "Would you believe there is a reward out for your rescue?"

The blonde woman grinned, "Well, I should hope so! How much is it? Our team has some discretionary funds for research, so we can pay you now, so you don't need to wait."

"It's 500 credits," Mila said, and then after a pause, "Each."

"No problem," the woman scientist responded, and she didn't seem to care how she spent Evo's money. Especially since Evo didn't seem to have launched a massive rescue for them.

The scientist tapped her navcomm against Mila's, and the two devices briefly lit up, but there was no sound to confirm the transfer. "Oh," she said, "Of course, there's no reception. I'm sure it will come through when we get topside."

"Thank you," Mila said. And since she was warming up to asking for things, she ventured, "I have a... friend... who is an Evo scientist. Her name is Bianca. Have you seen her here on Prema?"

The woman frowned, thinking.

"Hm... Is Bianca a geneticist? I met someone named Bianca here about a week ago–just for a minute in a meeting–before we got trapped, obviously–but I think I heard she was about to transferred off-world. I'm not sure where. Sorry."

"That's ok." Mila said, "It's nice to know she's doing well."

Mila made small talk, asking the scientists about their work. They were geologists trying to find new veins of a rare ore which helped specific plants grow faster when mixed in the soil. I wondered if I should ask them about the Ancient Tree on the spacestation, but I couldn't think of a way to bring it up discreetly. As we kept walking for another twenty minutes, the scientists fell into silence. The rhythms of our footsteps fell into time like a clock beat as we sloshed along the wastewater.

We eventually clambered out into the wider maintenance tunnel. We could now stand up with ease as we waited for the men to catch up. I discreetly found a piece of moss to connect with, so I could map out the fastest way above ground. I memorised the grid of tunnels. We weren't too far from an exit point.

The men caught up with us and stretched, relieved to stand upright after stooping in the tunnel. Everyone paused and drank some water.

"I think I'm going to cry when I see sunlight again," the reedy man stated, and everyone on the team murmured their agreement.

"This way," I directed, "Not long now."

We climbed up a ladder and entered another wide maintenance shaft, moving closer to the surface. As we stood on the landing, I heard a soft beep on Mila's navcomm. The money had transferred.

"Oh!" she cried, "We must have got reception!"

The team hooted in relief, and, with new energy, we began hiking towards the exit with more enthusiasm.

The women grinned as they took enthusiastic strides, but as I looked back behind me, I noticed the men hanging behind, peering at their navcomms. They had a heated but hushed exchange. I heard one say, "We just got an alert," and I met the gaze of one of the men. My stomach dropped as I realised something was wrong. They'd received some kind of message on their navcomm. And from the way they averted their gaze, I'd bet it was about us. If there wasn't a bounty on us when we landed on the planet, perhaps there was one now.

"Mila," I whispered, "What's going on?"

The reedy man reached into his back pocket and pull out a metallic object.

Mila turned to me, eyes wide. "It's a taser!" she cried. "*Run!*"

I met the eyes of the thin scientist, and his expression was one of determination. I began running. The blonde scientist leapt in front of the man with the taser. "What are you doing?!" she yelled, grabbing his wrist. But he shoved her out of the way. The woman with the glasses was pushed to the ground, her spectacles clattering out of reach.

Dimly, at the back of my awareness, a cry echoed off the tunnel walls: "Get them!"

I didn't wait. I ran. I knew how to run. I'd run barefoot in forests my entire life. Stride by stride, I ran, following Mila through the tunnel.

Out of the corner of my eye, taser fire flashed off a tunnel wall near me. The women were shouting, and there was a scream like someone had fallen. I didn't turn to look as the thump of solid boots was coming up behind me. They were taller than us and would catch up in no time with their longer stride.

As I ran, I noticed the walls were covered with moss. I reached out to it. Connecting, for just a second, I whispered, "*Help*". With that flash of electricity in my fingers, the moss started bubbling and racing down the side of the tunnel to cover the floor behind us, leaving a slippery, slimy trail.

"We're nearly there!" I cried to Mila, remembering the map I'd summoned earlier.

"Around this corner is an exit."

Mila found a ladder and started hauling herself up. A taser shot ripped past Mila's stomach and she yelped. At the heavy metal cover at the top, she cried in frustration, "It's stuck!"

"*You can lift it*!" I hissed through my teeth.

I turned behind me and saw the reedy man coming step-by-step closer. He raised his taser towards me. Mila pushed with all her weight to dislodge the cover. He slipped on the moss. Mila hauled herself out of the exit and I scrambled up the ladder.

As we threw ourselves out of the tunnel, we discovered we were in a patch of woods. It was night. We kept running.

I was hoping that we could get out of sight before they emerged from the tunnel. I didn't dare look behind me as we fled through the forest, leaping over fallen logs and crunching through the leaf litter. I paused and connected with a tree beside me and asked it to cover our tracks. Leaves from the forest rained down on our path. I bolted after Mila again, not wanting to lose sight of her.

We heard some shouts behind us, but they didn't sound like they were following us.

I didn't know where we were going, but I could see Mila glancing at her navcomm as she ran.

After a few minutes, I realised Mila's stride was off.

"Mila," I called, "Mila—did you get shot?"

"It's fine," she said, "Let's just get out of here."

"We've got a minute," I said, "I can't hear them. Can you?"

"No," she admitted.

"Let me look at it. I'm a healer."

She stopped, leaning against a tree to catch her breath. We were on the cusp of the desert. I could now see the side of her jumpsuit was singed. She started unbuttoning the jumpsuit and lifted up the singlet underneath. Above her hips was a scorch mark which was inflamed. I grabbed some aloe vera from my backpack and spread the sap across the burn. She sharply inhaled, her abs tightening as she winced.

"It would be better bandaged, but that will be okay for now," I said.

"Thanks," she said. "What the hell happened down there?"

"They got something on their navcomm about us. I heard the Evo scientists say that they wanted to get us!"

"Why would Evo want us? Did they find out about your powers?"

"No, I kept them a secret," I insisted, but my palms itched as I remembered the conversation I overheard Richard having with that woman on the spacestation after the blood test. *"We can get her back if the blood shows anything odd."* Is this what they meant?

"They took some of my blood," I confessed. "They were looking for markers or something."

"Geez, Addi. I don't need Evo paying attention to me right now!"

"Me!" I folded my arms. "Who says the alert wasn't about you! What if they found out that you broke into their computers?"

We stared at each other for a moment, mouths tight. But Mila smiled ruefully, "Maybe there's a bounty on *both* of us," she said. "We're well and truly screwed."

"What do we do now?"

Mila looked around at the night sky and across the desert. The high-speed train glowed in the distance as it made its way back to Claven city. The cold night air chilled my skin, now soaked in sweat and terror.

"Run. Hide," Mila shrugged, looking too exhausted to think.

I couldn't blame her. I couldn't believe what had happened over the last few days. I was on a planet so far from the life I knew. I had new powers I didn't know how to control. I had an Ancient One I needed to save. And we were being hunted by one of the largest corporations in the galaxy. I took a deep breath. It was one problem at a time, one day at a time.

Mila looked at her navcomm. "Well, the good news is we've got enough credits to get off the planet and find somewhere to lie low."

"Sounds good," I said.

"That is—if you want to stick together?"

"I think we're in this together," I said, "Besides, I think we make a pretty good team,"

"Yeah, we do."

"But first things first: let's get to the *Scout* and get off this planet."

She pointed across the desert to the train stop, a soft yellow light glowing on the platform. We started running across the wasteland, step-by-step, leaving a trail of messy footprints in the red dirt behind us.

***

What happens next?

Start *Sapling's Aurora* now...

What happens next?

Can Addi get a handle on her new powers? Will Mila be able to find Bianca? And why are Evo is hunting them?

Find out in the next book, *Sapling's Aurora,* out now.

Scan to grab the next book:

Did you enjoy *Sapling's Orbit*?

Did you love Addi's first steps offworld and Mila's kick-ass attitude? Were you hooked by their budding connection? Can't wait to find out more about super-creepy Evo corporation? And that is going on with that tree?!

Share your love for *Sapling's Orbit* and tell your friends to get on board the *Scout*.

Leave a review on Storygraph, Goodreads, your socials, or wherever you bought the book.

About the author

Spencer Rose is a writer from Sydney, Australia. She writes in the early morning, with a strong coffee or two, often at a café. When not writing, she enjoys hiking, playing video games, crafting and baking. Visit her online at spencerrosewrites.com or on Instagram or TikTok at @spencerrosewrites.